THE WIDOW'S CABIN

L.G. DAVIS

The Widow's Cabin
L.G. Davis
Copyright © 2020
All Rights Reserved.

For Simon

CHAPTER 1

⌒

In less than a year, my husband will be gone. Forever. He will not only be leaving me behind, but also the world.

That's why every second counts.

Brett's hand is warm against my palm. He's trying to comfort me. I hate that he's failing at it. But I smile because I'm trying to comfort him right back. I'm probably failing too.

Every day of my life, I wake up each morning waiting for the other shoe to drop.

Being dragged from one foster family to the next as a kid only to be returned *to sender* time and time again does that to you.

Brett was my new beginning, my fairytale. But fairytales don't exist, not in my world. I was a fool to believe they did.

The early years of our marriage were tough. I loved Brett, but I struggled to be close to him, to be happy. It had a lot to do with his father.

Once I had finally become accustomed to

living with my pain and had learned how to fake happiness, cancer struck.

I'm trying hard to be strong for both of us, but I'm slowly coming undone.

"Are you okay?" Brett lifts a thick eyebrow. His voice is deep with exhaustion.

Since his stomach cancer diagnosis one month ago, he tires more easily. That doesn't stop him from giving the little energy he has left to the Black Oyster Resort, one of his father's hotels that's based in Fort Haven, North Carolina.

That's where we met. His father had hired me to work as a maid, and Brett and I fell in love and got married within six months.

Business always comes first for Brett, even before our little family. Whenever I confront him, he denies it, but it's the truth. I thought I was okay with getting the scraps of his time. I forced myself to be grateful for having him in my life at all. Not anymore, though, not when we have such little time left together.

It's our wedding anniversary and I had wanted us to create one last happy memory. Tonight, I had wanted to live in denial, to pretend our life is perfect even when it's far from it.

His phone beeps before I can respond, before I can go on fooling myself.

The other shoe drops. I expected it to.

Brett always answers his calls, especially when it's his father. Every time that man calls, he jumps.

I reach for his hand and squeeze it. "Don't," I whisper, knowing full well that I'm asking for the impossible. "Don't answer it, please."

His gaze moves to the phone nestled between his glass of sparkling water and his empty plate.

"Sorry, sweetheart. It's my father. You know I have to." He wipes his mouth and tosses his napkin onto the table, then reaches for the phone to speak to my father-in-law, the man who controls both our lives.

Cole Wilton calls himself a father, but he's not. He's far worse than a dictator, who treats his son like a puppet and everyone else like trash. In his presence, Brett is always anxious and helpless. While I do my best to build him up, his father never misses a chance to make him feel small.

I wish so much I could help Brett see what a snake his father is. Cole knows he's not welcome in our home. It's the only place Brett can be himself without the cloud of his father's disapproval hovering over him. It's the only place I can feel safe.

Cole shows up anyway from time to time,

reminding us that the luxury two-story house we live in belongs to him.

My most terrifying encounter with him was the night before I married Brett. He made it clear to me that he did not approve of me marrying his son and made a promise to destroy our marriage if I didn't call off the wedding. I went ahead and married Brett anyway, but nothing was ever the same. Cole poisoned our marriage before it even started.

After the wedding, I was desperate to get away, and I begged Brett to walk away from Fort Haven so we could start a new life in another town.

I even proposed that we move to another Black Oyster Hotel location, so he could continue to work in the family business. Brett dismissed the idea immediately. His father needed him in Fort Haven, he claimed. The truth is that his father wanted to have him close enough to control.

Blowing out a frustrated breath, I fold up my own napkin and push myself to my feet. While Brett is on the phone, I head upstairs to check on Liam.

I meet Janella at the top of the sweeping stairs.

"Liam sleeping already," she whispers, her face blank as always.

At thirty-five, Janella is three years older than me, but she already has noticeable wrinkles at the corners of her dark brown eyes and around her pinched mouth. In spite of all of that, she's a stunning woman with big eyes and lashes that don't need mascara to make them stand out. The dark goddess braid she always wears to work and the elegant way she moves make her look royal in my eyes. I only wish she would smile more to light up her face.

Janella came before me. When I moved in, she was already the Wiltons' housekeeper.

Even though I would have personally hired someone more cheerful, I couldn't find it in me to let her go. Something about her pulled at my heartstrings. She kind of reminded me of myself. The pain I knew she carried inside her heart connected with mine. She never said much about herself, but sometimes I feel connected to her somehow. Like me, she's intimidated by Cole. Every time he shows up at the house, her shoulders hunch and she flinches when he speaks.

She's also great at her job and always goes above and beyond, sometimes even taking on the role of a nanny to our four-year-old son, Liam. I tell her often that looking after Liam is not part of her job, but she insists that she likes to keep busy.

I only wish I could communicate with her more. Since she speaks only a little English, we use a lot of sentence fragments and sign language to get the message across.

What I know is that she's alone in the US while her family is in the Philippines and she needs to support them on her own. Since she takes on so many tasks around the house and helps me with Liam, I told Brett to increase her salary, but he informed me that it was Cole who paid her.

It gets to me to know that Cole has so much control over our lives. That night Brett and I had an argument that lasted for hours. Many more followed that one, all having something to do with his father, but we always came back to the same place, right where we started, underneath Cole's thumb. Brett was never going to stand up to him and demand his freedom. There were many times I resented him for it, but my love for him made me stay. He needed me. He needs me.

"Thank you. It's best I don't disturb him, then," I tell Janella and she nods. "You can go home now. Go and rest."

She nods and for a moment she gazes at my face, as if studying it. "Good sleep, Mrs. Wilton," she says finally, and I sigh with relief. I was starting to become uncomfortable under her intense stare.

"Good night, Janella."

Instead of returning downstairs, I head over to our bedroom and sit on the edge of the bed, my hands pressed into the comforter. My chin rests on my chest, my eyes burning with unshed tears.

I try not to think about how our lives will be when Brett is no longer here.

Brett lives each day pretending the cancer is not real. He prefers to live in denial. Every time I mention it, he checks out of the conversation. He hasn't even told his father about it and he made me promise not to either.

I wish he would fight for his life, but he refuses to do chemotherapy, even though the doctors claim he might add a few more months or even years to his thirty-six. Brett's reasoning is that there's no guarantee that it will work.

There's more to it. He knows that treatment might weaken him, and if there's one thing Brett hates, it's to display any weakness, especially in front of his father. Cole has everything to do with many of the decisions Brett makes.

A soft knock on the door forces me to raise my head.

Brett is standing in the doorway, his phone in his hand. "I'm sorry," he says. "I have to go to the hotel. There's an emergency."

Brett once told me that as a child, his dream was to become a doctor. Thanks to Cole forcing him to join the family business, his dream didn't come true. I never fail to see the regret etched in his features when he plays doctor games with Liam, where one of them is a patient and the other the doctor.

He may not have become a doctor, but sometimes he lives the life of a doctor. He gets a call and a few minutes later he's gone. It doesn't matter what time of night it is.

"What kind of emergency?" I ask, feeling deflated.

"Employee issues. Nothing that can't be sorted out."

"Did someone else quit?" In the past month, two housekeepers have resigned. I understand why they would. Working for a controlling man like Cole is not easy.

"Yeah." Brett rubs the back of his neck. He looks so tired and I want to draw him into my arms, but I'm also annoyed with him.

"Can't your father handle it?" I don't understand why Cole always feels the need to call Brett. He lives in a spacious luxury suite at the hotel. He should be able to handle issues immediately without help.

"No. It's something only I can handle." He

shoves his phone into his pocket. "I won't be long. I promise." He crosses the room and comes to kiss the tip of my nose. In the past, his kisses used to offer me comfort, but now I barely feel anything.

"Don't be long," I call after him. "I'll wait up for you."

The door closes behind him and a few minutes later, his Range Rover roars to life.

I remain sitting on my bed listening to the silence, my eyes closed. Then I fall back onto the bed and fall asleep in my pretty canary yellow cocktail dress.

Brett wakes me up when he enters the room, his curly dark hair as rumpled as his shirt.

The first thing I do is glance at the clock. It's five minutes to midnight. He left at eight.

"Hey." If he didn't have cancer, I would start an argument. I'm dying to, but he already looks so tired and his eyes look empty and broken. He probably had a fight with his father.

He doesn't respond as he walks over to his side of the bed and removes his socks.

"Was it something serious?" I ask, going to massage his shoulders. I'm surprised when he flinches a little.

He gets to his feet and my hands drop from his shoulders. "Yeah," he says and disappears into the massive closet. He remains there for almost fifteen minutes. Figuring that he needs to be alone to recover from whatever pain his father inflicted on him, I give him the space. I change into my nightgown and wait patiently for him under the covers in case he wants to talk.

When he exits the closet, he's wearing his pajamas and the expression on his face is even darker than before. For a few heartbeats, he stands in the middle of the room and stares at me.

"What's wrong, Brett? You're scaring me. Did you have an argument with your father?"

He nods and finally climbs into bed. He doesn't explain and I don't ask him. I don't think I want to know. Hearing the things Cole calls his son disgusts me.

I hate Cole even more for ruining our anniversary. He might even have invented the emergency so he could destroy Brett's plans for the evening. Maybe that's why Brett is so furious.

I rest my head on his chest, listening to his heartbeat, wondering how many of them are still left before his heart stops forever.

"I need you to promise me one thing."

"Okay," I whisper and hold my breath.

"Don't let the cancer eat me alive," he says in a choked voice.

"What...what are you saying?" I sit up and search his eyes. They're blank.

"When it gets to be too much, when I'm too weak, I want you…" Words fail him as he bites his lip, still staring ahead. "Help me die with dignity."

After hearing his words, for what feels like an hour, I can't move or breathe.

"Did you hear me?" he asks, finally looking at me.

"No." I shake my head, tears spilling from my eyes. "I don't understand."

"You do." He turns me to face him and gazes deep into my eyes. "When I reach the end, I want you to help me die."

"You want me to kill you?" I'm shocked that those words are even leaving my lips.

"I want you to help me. If you really love me, you will do it."

CHAPTER 2

༄

I press my ear to the wooden door, straining to hear the conversation happening in the kitchen between Brett and his father.

It's been two months since Brett asked me to do the unthinkable, and I'm still reeling with shock, especially since the day after, he told me exactly how he wanted to die. He said he wanted to die on his own terms. He didn't want cancer to win.

I listened without interrupting him, praying that he would change his mind.

I don't know if he has changed his mind because he barely says a word to me anymore. His health is deteriorating at the same rate as his mood.

Even though he's still here, it feels like he's already gone. He has even distanced himself from Liam. It kills me to watch him ignoring our son.

Sometimes I think he's pulling away to try

and prepare us for a life without him.

Almost every day I beg Brett to accept treatment that might extend his life, but he shuts down every conversation about the topic.

Much as I'd rather shut Cole out of our lives and hate to see him around my husband when he's so fragile, maybe he's the only person Brett will listen to.

Brett begged me not to tell his father about his illness, but Cole found out anyway. For all I know, it was Brett who told him. Or he could have seen the signs of illness in Brett, whose weight has melted off and whose eyes and cheeks have sunken into his skull.

He burst into our house just as we were finishing up with dinner.

"You will fight this thing like a man," he barks at Brett. "Are you a man or some wimp?"

I press my back against the wall next to the kitchen door and squeeze my eyes shut. The force of Cole's harsh words bruises even me.

Cole doesn't love his son. The only reason he wants Brett to fight cancer is that he wants to keep emotionally abusing him. He derives power from crushing his son. But right now, I want Brett to live and I'm praying Cole will get through to him.

"You have no right to tell me what and what I cannot do about my health. I know you like to have your way, but not this time." Brett's words are edged with steel. "I need you to get out of this house. I thought I made it clear that you're no longer welcome here."

I hear something smash and my heart jumps to my throat. "How dare you speak to me in that manner!" Cole grinds the words out between his teeth. "You stupid boy. This house and everything you think you own belong to me."

A part of me is proud that Brett is finally standing up to his father and telling him to go to hell. It's something I have begged him to do for years. But this time it's not for the right reasons.

"Fine. Then we'll find another place to live." Brett coughs then laughs. "You still think you control me, don't you? Guess what, you don't, Cole. It's over. I'm done with you and your pathetic hotels. I'm out for good. I no longer want to be a part of anything to do with you." He pauses. "And you know what, before I leave this world, I'm going to do the right thing. I'll show the world what you really are. We'll get out of this house by morning."

"The hell you will," Cole booms. "You will stay here, and you will fight this thing. You've lived your life trying to prove to me that you're a man. Now's the time to show it. I'll send some doctors to come and see you tomorrow. You will undergo chemo and that's the end of it."

I don't see it, but I imagine Brett shriveling up in his chair, looking like the scared little boy I'd seen in one of his few childhood photos.

I expect him to respond, but instead, the door flies open and Cole storms out. It's too late for me to make an escape.

His slate-gray eyes are like hot pools of fury when they meet mine, and a muscle is quivering in his jaw. "We need to talk," he barks, and I step away from him before I'm scorched by his anger. "Follow me to the office." He has a slight limp when he walks. Brett told me it was from an accident he had as a child.

Talking to Cole in private is something I try my best to avoid. The last time we were alone in a room was the day before I married Brett. But this time it's a matter of life and death, so, I follow him to the office. However, the moment we reach the room, I decide not to enter.

"What do you want to talk about?" I ask from the doorway.

"Take a seat," he orders as he rubs his upturned nose.

He doesn't sit down. He prefers to tower over people, to make them feel small. The fifty-six-year-old man uses his tall and athletic height of at least six feet, three inches to intimidate.

I jam my hands into my armpits to stop them from shaking. "I prefer to stand. You wanted to talk, so talk."

For a moment I think he will explode, but instead, he eyes me through his hooded gaze, his lips spread into a creepy thin-lipped smile.

I sigh inwardly when he drops into Brett's desk chair. "You should have told me as soon as he was diagnosed."

"Brett asked me not to. He's my husband and I respect his wishes."

"He's my son, damn you. You should have told me. I knew from the start that you were bad news."

I drop my hands to my sides and curl them into fists of rage. I want to shoot him a scathing remark, but the words freeze inside my throat as they often do in a conversation with him. "It's not... you know—"

He wraps a hand around his left wrist, covering his gold Rolex. "You will force him to undergo chemo. No son of mine will be terrified of treatment. I didn't raise a coward. You turned him into that."

I bite into my lip hard, so I don't lash out at him. This is not about me. It's about Brett. "I don't know if I can promise you that. I've tried for a month and failed."

"I'm not asking you, Meghan. I'm telling you. I'll fly in some of the best doctors in the country. They will be here tomorrow. Make sure Brett is home." His face is hard as he pushes to his feet and charges toward the door. I move out of the way before he gets too close.

Without another word to me, he strides out, and a few seconds later, he's gone. I remain inside the office for a few minutes, drawing in calming breaths before I have to face Brett again. He has become such an angry man that being with him drains me of energy.

Once I have collected myself, I go and dismiss Janella for the day. She only nods and leaves quietly. I didn't fail to notice that when Cole showed up, as usual, she made herself disappear.

After tucking Liam in, I search for Brett. I find him already in bed, trembling under the covers, his face contorted with pain. I'm used to seeing him in pain now since it's something that's become more and more a part of our lives, but this time it's different, more intense.

He's writhing under the covers, and his face is covered in a sheen of sweat. For a moment his eyes bulge as if they're about to pop out of his head. He's gazing in my direction, but he doesn't seem to be seeing me. His father's visit must have hurt him more than I thought.

"Baby, I'm sorry you're in so much pain." I lie down next to him, putting my arms around his frail body. He tries to push me away, but whenever he's in pain, I'm the stronger one.

"I'll get you some meds." I slide off the bed.

"No," he grunts. "No painkiller." His lips seem to have gone blue and his eyes are pleading with me to respect his wish.

"You need help, baby. I'll take you to the hospital, okay?" I search the room for my handbag, because that's where my phone is.

"No hospital." This time his tone is hard, final. Then his face crumples with pain again, his eyes squeezed tight. "Help me. *You* help me."

I want to pretend I don't know what he's talking about, but in between the grunts of pain, he spells it out for me.

"I want you to...help...die."

I run back to the bed. "No, Brett." I cup his sweating face with both hands. My eyes are so blurred that I can barely see his features. "Don't ask me to do that to you."

"Please." He becomes a weeping mess. It kills me inside to see a grown man, my husband, crying like a child, and I cannot give him the kind of help he wants.

He continues to beg, but his voice has sunk

to a whisper. His gaze is distant again as if he's looking right through me, as if he's already dying.

"I want to die." I can hear every word as if he were speaking in a loud voice.

"Okay." I pull away from him as he curls up into a ball. "Okay." Tears are pouring down my face and I don't bother to wipe them away. What's the point when they will only be replaced by more?

"Thank you," he says as I walk out of the room and head down to the kitchen.

Before I open the medicine cabinet, a sound I can't place catches my attention. I will my heart to stop pounding so I can make it out, but it refuses.

I glance out the window and decide that it must be the branches outside hitting the wall. Some of the trees are getting too big and need pruning.

I shut the blinds and get back to what I'm planning to do. I back away from the medicine cabinet and grab the counter with my hands, my fingers curling around the slab of marble. Janella has forgotten her cell phone. It lies neglected on the counter, but it's not important right now.

I reach for a dish towel and press it against my eyes, then I pull in a breath and shut off my emotions. The only thought in my mind is giving Brett relief so I never have to see him in that much pain again.

The night he explained to me how he wanted to die, he also told me about a brown paper package in the medicine cabinet with everything I would need to end his life. I never looked inside it until now.

There's also a page with instructions. I follow them to perfection.

The filled syringe is light, but it feels heavy in my hand. I don't even know what kind of medication he wants me to inject into his body because the packaging is plain white.

As I follow the instructions, I'm not thinking anymore, my fingers moving as if they're detached from my body.

Once the syringe is filled with the milky liquid, I pour him a glass of whiskey as he requested, his last drink on Earth. In a daze, I take everything upstairs.

I let myself into the room and lock the door behind me. In the few minutes I was away, his body seems to have shriveled up. He's trembling now as if he's having a seizure. Holding the whiskey in one hand and the syringe in the other, I shuffle to the bed. Tears are still burning their way down my cheeks.

Once he stops trembling so much, I find the

courage to approach the bed and sit next to him.

I offer to help him put the whiskey to his lips, but he mouths *no*. "Do it," he croaks. "Plea...please."

He's asking me to do the worst thing I have ever done in my life. He told me that the medication he chose will be undetectable in the body if an autopsy is carried out. He said they will never know how he died and would probably think it's the illness that took him.

He's too weak to even raise his hand. The moment I wrap my hand around his wrist and feel his pulse, I'm catapulted back to my senses.

What am I doing? What am I about to do right now?

"No." I drop his hand again. "No," I repeat.

I have a son. Euthanasia is considered murder. I'm about to commit murder. I can't do it. It's wrong.

Brett tries to reach for my hand, but he can barely lift his hand and his body has started to quake again, saliva sliding down his cheek.

The syringe falls from my hand and drops to the floor next to the nightstand. Instead of picking it up, I get to my feet and gaze down from him to it.

"What are you doing?" he whispers. His lips look lifeless even in the warm light of the lamp.

"I love you. I don't want to kill you. It's murder. I'm sorry, but I can't. I love you." I charge to the door and unlock it. I need to get away from him before I can change my mind and do something stupid. I need to catch my breath.

He's calling me, but his voice is too weak to make out his words. I don't stop until I'm safely in the office. I fling open the windows so the June breeze can flood in, then I drop into the desk chair.

CHAPTER 3

～

He's my husband, the father of my son. It's killing me to watch cancer eat away at him, but I don't have the right to play God, and he has no right to ask me to.

I need to stop hiding inside his office. I should go and share my decision with him. But I can't bring myself to stand.

The leather squeaks as I lean forward to push my head between my knees. Tears slide down the insides of my calves and onto my bare feet. Some fall onto the oak wooden floor to form perfect liquid marbles.

I press my knees against my ears, but I can't shut out the sounds. I can still hear his tortured groans as he begs me to set him free.

I get to my feet, but I'm swaying as if I've had a bit too much to drink. Caring for Brett the past two months has taken a toll on me. The fact that he has been so angry and distant makes it even worse. He needs me and pushes me away at the same time.

He might never forgive me for denying him his last wish, but he's asking too much. Giving him what he wants could destroy me. By setting him free from the pain, I will possibly be dooming myself to prison. If I end up there, our son will be left without either of his parents to raise him.

Cole would probably step in to raise him. The thought disgusts me. I despise the man and everything he stands for. I won't let him raise my son the way he raised his son, treating him like his puppet.

Liam needs one of us to protect him from monsters like his grandfather.

Determined, I force myself to move forward. The door feels like it's miles away, but I make it without fainting.

My feet feel heavy as I climb the stairs.

I no longer hear Brett crying. The large house feels eerily quiet except for everyday sounds that have become familiar to the point that I no longer hear them. The distant sound of the clock ticking and the fridge humming as I walk past the kitchen door.

One. Two. Three.

Thirteen steps take me to the top of the staircase.

I pass Liam's door. It's slightly open. In my

confused state, I must have forgotten to close it fully when I checked on him earlier.

For a moment, I stand in front of it, my hand on the door handle, then I take a breath and close it softly.

I shuffle to the master bedroom and come to a halt again. I'm afraid to enter, to see my husband writhing in agony.

A trickle of sweat trails its way down my left temple. I don't bother to wipe it away.

You can do this, I tell myself.

Until now, I have respected Brett's decision not to seek treatment, but I can't do it anymore. I'll have to plead with him to allow me to call 911. The pain is killing him, and he is refusing painkillers.

He needs to be rushed to the hospital.

My palm is slippery against the metal handle, making it harder to turn it. It finally gives in and the door swings open.

The room is the way I left it, but something feels different somehow and I can't place my finger on it.

Brett is still in bed, but the shaking has stopped.

I'm relieved that the pain has left him and he's sleeping now, but I also feel guilty for leaving him alone when he needed me most. But I couldn't stay. I couldn't give him what he wanted. I needed a moment to pull myself together, to think.

My gaze moves to the carpet and my blood runs cold. The syringe is right next to the bed where I dropped it, but even from where I'm standing, I can see that it's empty. The thick, off-white liquid is gone.

My throat starts to close up and I stumble back.

He couldn't have. Did he find the strength to do it himself? But he was so weak and barely able to speak.

My back slams against the closed door and my hand clutches my chest.

I'm afraid to approach the bed, afraid of what I might find.

I haven't noticed before, but the room is quiet even though my husband snores. The comforter also isn't moving, which means his chest is not rising and falling. He's not breathing.

Was he so desperate for death that he decided to take his own life?

If he's dead, I could still be held responsible. I prepared the deadly cocktail and sucked it into the syringe. I had brought it upstairs intending to do what he wanted me to do because it was too devastating to watch a grown man cry.

Or maybe I'm wrong and he's fine. I need to see for certain. I place one foot in front of the other until I reach the bed. My hands are clenched so tight that my nails dig into my palm.

"Brett," I say in a broken whisper. "Brett," I repeat when he doesn't respond.

Fear gushing through my veins, I reach out and touch him.

I don't want to believe what my mind is telling me, but the truth is staring me straight in the face. Brett is not moving.

When I finally find the courage to look at his face, I see that it's pale and colorless. His eyes are closed.

My hand claps my mouth to stifle a scream, which turns to groans deep inside my throat. Even before feeling his pulse, I know he's gone.

But what if by some miracle, there's a pulse and the doctors can revive him?

My heart lodged inside my throat, I run to my side of the bed and grab my phone.

When I try to press the numbers, it slides from my hands and falls at my feet, but I snatch it up and dial 911, something I should have done when Brett was in pain.

The dispatcher promises that the paramedics will be at the house in fifteen minutes. In the meantime, I'm instructed to stay on the phone and to perform CPR. I turn on the speaker and try to bring my husband back. I don't succeed.

Before opening the door to the paramedics, I grab the syringe and push it into a hidden pocket in my handbag. What I'm doing would be considered a crime, but the fear of going to prison is unbearable.

If he's gone, it won't matter how the poison entered his body. If I had not mixed it for him, he would not be lying in bed lifeless.

But Brett was the one who got the medication. He was the one who told me how to mix it when the time came. He promised me that the poison would be undetectable, so I had nothing to worry about, but I am worried.

And very heartbroken.

The clock is ticking too slowly, so I try to resuscitate him the way I've seen people do on TV. All the while I talk to him as my tears drip onto his face.

He doesn't answer and still doesn't move.

He doesn't smile. He doesn't blink.

He's not breathing.

It's too late. He's not coming back, the small voice inside my head taunts.

I refuse to listen to it.

I press my forehead against his and beg him

not to leave.

"Please, Brett, don't do this to me. I need you. Liam needs you. Baby, please open your eyes." I lie next to him and hold him tight.

When the paramedics arrive, they confirm my worst fears. I tell them about his cancer and how he was in so much pain.

"I found him dead." I hope they won't read the truth from my eyes. "I came upstairs, and he was–" I break down then, and they can't get me to say anything more. More questions will come later, and I don't know if I'll be able to stick to my story.

Cole arrives while I watch Brett's corpse being taken away. I don't even remember calling him. Maybe I did without even knowing it. Or maybe he was on his way over anyway. When the paramedics tell him what happened, he sinks onto the front steps and says nothing for a long time.

As soon as they leave, I stumble into the house. Before I can close the door, he slams it open and charges in. I don't want him anywhere near me or my son, but it's his house and if I lock him out, he has a key to let himself back in.

I try to walk away from him to go and check on Liam, but he grabs my arm hard and spins me around.

I yank my arm from his grip and massage away the discomfort.

"You killed him," he accuses me with so much conviction that for a moment I'm terrified that he knows what happened.

"No." I shake my head as tears flood my throat. "He was sick and—"

"You wanted him to die sooner so you can take his money. That's why you talked him out of getting treatment. Tell me I'm wrong."

"You are wrong, and for you to think I could do such a thing is disgusting. My husband is dead. I'm sure you'll understand that I want to be alone."

"You won't be for long. I can assure you of that. Soon enough the cops will show up with questions. The truth will come to the light and you will pay for this, you piece of trash."

"Get the hell out," I shout, forgetting it's his house. "I need you to leave or—"

"Or you'll call the cops? They're already on their way. I called them."

"Mommy, what happened?" Liam's voice brings our argument to a screeching halt.

I throw Cole a warning look and take Liam back to bed. "Grandpa was just leaving, baby. Let me go and read you a story."

"Make it a good one," Cole says as we climb the stairs.

CHAPTER 4

I'm standing at Liam's bedroom window after he finally falls asleep again when voices float upstairs.

Even though Cole had pretended to leave earlier, he hadn't. I could see him waiting in his car. I've been watching him from the window, wishing he would leave me alone.

I'm not surprised that he wants to be around when the cops question me. He's determined to destroy me.

I don't think he even cares if I killed my husband or not. He wants me to pay for disobeying him, for going ahead and marrying his son when he asked me not to. He did tell me then that I would regret my decision.

I'm terrified of going downstairs. I feel safer in Liam's room. But if I don't go down, if I don't go and answer their questions, they might think I'm guilty.

Brokenhearted, I watch Liam stir in his

sleep. I pray he won't wake up before the cops leave. I also pray he doesn't wake up to find both his mom and dad gone.

Holding my breath, I tiptoe across the room to face the cops before Cole comes to get me.

I feel physically sick as I close the door again and drag myself to the stairs.

One of the cops is already making his way up the stairs. I recognize him as Officer Robert Kane. He's a tall, heavyset man with graying mouse-brown hair. His warm, green eyes and laugh lines don't fool me. He's Cole's friend, which makes him my enemy.

When a crime is committed in Fort Haven, he's usually the one interviewed on the local news. He seems to always enjoy his local celebrity.

The thing that makes my insides twist with anxiety is the fact that I used to see him come to the Black Oyster to visit Cole. I'm sure Cole has already fed his police friend all the lies that would give me a one-way ticket to prison.

"Good evening, Mrs. Wilton," Officer Kane says. "I'm very sorry for your loss. Do you think you can answer some questions? I'm afraid it's routine."

I can feel Cole's eyes on me from down below. He's trying to intimidate me from a distance, so I'll mess up my story and set a trap for myself.

I nod and wipe the tears from my cheeks. Even though I'm trembling inside, I do my best to pull myself together and steel myself for his questions.

I follow Officer Kane down the stairs, where Cole is standing by the window with his arms folded. As a member of the family, I don't understand why he is not also being questioned by the police.

Another officer is studying a multi-colored abstract painting on the wall, one I have never understood. I was never allowed to change any of the furniture, so most of the decorations do not even appeal to my taste. It was the price we had to pay for staying in Cole's house.

Cole offers the officers a seat and I lower myself into an armchair not far from where he's sitting. I want to cry and weep, but I just feel numb inside. The pain will return later, but now I'm glad to feel nothing. It enables me to think straight and say the right things.

"Mrs. Wilton, your father-in-law, filled us in on what happened, but I would like to hear it from your perspective. You were the one with your husband in the house, is that correct?"

I nod. "Yes, it is." I can't believe this is happening. I cannot believe I'm being questioned about my husband's death, that I'm in this situation at all.

Before I answer, I look past the officer's shoulders at Cole. He's still standing by the window, staring at me, waiting for the officer to break me with his questions.

I always used to think hate is a strong word, but nothing else can describe the crawling sensation of disgust I feel when my eyes meet Cole's. Now that Brett is gone, I don't have to hide my hate. I don't have to bury it deep inside as a way to protect him.

I want Cole to know exactly how much I'm disgusted by him.

I take a breath and tell the officer the same story I told the paramedics. I paint the scene as it was in the moments that turned my life upside down. That I was helping Brett get into bed when pain overcame his body, stomach cramps that made him cry out with agony, and that I left the room for a few minutes, and when I returned, I found him dead.

"All lies," Cole's voice booms behind me. "Look at her, she's a liar. She's always been a liar. She lied about loving my son. She was only interested in his money."

I want to lash out at him, but I need to keep control. I need to keep my anger in check before I blow my cover.

Yes, it's all lies, but the truth can never come

out in the open. I was the only one there. I'm the only one whose story matters. As long as the police do not uncover any other evidence that could contradict my story, I will not go to prison.

If they knew that I even thought of helping Brett to die, I would be right in the center of a murder case. Everyone in Fort Haven would know about it since Brett and Cole are so well-known around town. I will be on the news and in the papers. I will be called a murderer.

"Mr. Wilton, if you don't mind, I would like to speak to Mrs. Wilton alone."

"I don't understand why that is necessary. I might have some of the answers she's not giving you."

"I appreciate that, but she was here when it happened. We only need a few minutes. I hope you don't mind."

Cole's eyes blaze as he gazes at Officer Kane. At first, I think he is going to refuse to leave the room, but I sigh with relief when he clears his throat and walks out. Instead of heading upstairs, he goes outside, probably to smoke one of his many cigars.

"How long has your husband been sick for?" Officer Kane asks me.

"He was diagnosed with cancer three months ago. He was okay for one month, but the last two months were... It was hard."

"And you say he refused treatment?"

"Yes. The doctors recommended chemotherapy, but he completely refused it. I tried to convince him to do it, but he wouldn't." I glance out the floor-to-ceiling window at the darkness outside. I haven't checked the time, but it must be close to 3:00 or 4:00 a.m. I'm not sure, honestly. Everything is either moving too fast or in slow motion right now. "He was in so much pain...tonight," I murmur, then I glance back at the officer, who is still jotting down my words onto his notepad.

I wish I could cry for relief and also to convince the officer that I am grieving my dead husband. I don't want him to believe Cole, that I married Brett for his money. With Cole holding the purse strings, I would probably not even get a penny.

"What was his outlook?" the other officer asks. Only then do I notice that he's quite young, probably no older than twenty-five, but the police uniform makes him look older.

"The doctors gave him less than a year to live unless he underwent treatment."

"Do you know why he refused treatment?"

I shake my head. "But I saw on his computer that he researched stories about people who underwent chemotherapy and most of those people either died or it failed to work. I guess he didn't want to be disappointed." I don't share with him that in his search history, I also found search results for 'the quickest ways to die'.

"Was there any medication he was taking to manage the pain?" the younger officer asks.

"He did have medication, but tonight he refused to take it."

"Why do you think that is?" Officer Kane asks, his brow furrowing. "Why didn't he want the pain meds?"

"I don't know. He just refused."

"And he also refused to go to the hospital?"

"Yes." I pinch the bridge of my nose. "There was nothing I could do to help him."

The second officer comes to sit down on the couch as well and leans forward. I raise my gaze to meet his brown eyes. "You mentioned that you left the room for a few minutes. Why? Why would you leave your husband when he's in pain?"

I bite into my lip for a moment, trying to straighten out my story before I shoot myself in the foot. Then I take a breath. "Because I couldn't stand it. He was my husband and I could not stand seeing him in so much pain. I needed a moment."

"That's understandable," Officer Kane says and I almost sigh with relief that he bought my story. But then again, that part of the story was not hard to tell because it was true.

The younger officer pushes himself to his feet and leaves the room to step outside. Maybe he wants to ask Cole questions as well.

"Mrs. Wilton, I know this is hard," I can hear in Officer Kane's voice that he means it.

"Thank you." He gives me a moment to catch my breath before he continues.

"When you left the room, where did you go?"

"I went to the office."

The next thing he wants is for me to take him there. I don't understand why it's important, but I don't resist. I need to play along.

The first thing I see when we enter are the papers spread out on the desk. Cole doesn't know it, but since marrying Brett, I had been helping him out with the Black Oyster financial reports. Even though I didn't go to college, I'm quite good with numbers. During Brett's illness, I took on more of the CFO tasks, so his father didn't think he was slacking.

Yesterday morning, while taking a short break, I was working on the business plan for the bakery I was planning to open up in a few weeks. Now I can't help but feel that that dream, along with many others, is about to go up in smoke.

"So, you were in here?" he asks, looking around him. "Were you sitting or standing?"

I throw him a confused look. "Is that important?"

"I'm afraid so. Please answer the question."

Don't annoy him, I tell myself.

"At first I was pacing the room and then I sat in that chair." I point to the leather chair. My gaze moves to the floor in front of it and I imagine my tears dripping onto the wood. "I was crying. Maybe that's why I left the room. I didn't want him to see me cry. I wanted to be strong for him, but at that moment, I couldn't be."

"How long have you been married to Mr. Wilton again?"

"Five years." I still don't understand why that is relevant, but I answer anyway.

"How did you meet?"

"I was employed at the Black Oyster Hotel. That's where I met him."

"Was he the one who hired you?"

"No, it was his father." Ice spreads through my stomach when I think of the day that changed my life, the moment I accepted the position at the Black Oyster Hotel. How could

I have known that it would end like this?

A moment passes while he writes down everything. Then he glances up again. "How long did you date before you got married?"

"Less than a year."

"Can you be more specific?"

I sigh. "Around three months."

I can see that the officer is judging me as he studies my face.

"We were very much in love," I say, adding to my statement, so he doesn't come to his own conclusions.

"Was your father-in-law correct in claiming you married Brett Wilton for his money?"

My throat closes up and the urge to lash out is so strong, it awakens cramps in my belly, but instead, I straighten my shoulders and look him straight in the eye. "I did not marry my husband for his money." I do not tell him that I did love to move into a comfortable life and to never have to worry about where next month's rent money was coming from. "If you think I killed him, why would I do that? Why didn't I just wait for the illness to take him?"

"That's not what I'm thinking, Mrs. Wilton." He pauses. "I'm sorry if I made you feel that way. I need to have a complete picture. I truly am sorry for your loss."

"Thank you." I sniff and wrap my arms

around myself for warmth. I hadn't even noticed until now that I'm still wearing my nightgown.

"I think we have everything we need for now, but we might return if we come up with any more questions." He pushes his notebook into his breast pocket. "And I'm sorry, but there will probably be an investigation because we need to rule out foul play."

"I understand." My voice comes out strained and broken as fear digs its claws into my spine.

After the questioning, Cole no longer comes inside but talks to both officers outside. Then all of them get into their cars and drive away.

Instead of heading upstairs, I remain in the living room. I don't dare to go to the bedroom where Brett died.

I fight my anxiety for an hour until I give in and swallow down some of my pills. I wonder how many more of them I will take in the next couple of days, weeks, or even months. I wonder if they will be able to shield me from the storm that I sense is coming.

CHAPTER 5

༄

I need to get out of the house. The memories of what happened last night are suffocating me. I barely got any sleep, and I'm still lying on the couch, unable to move.

Finally, I push myself up, almost falling to my knees. For a moment I stand, hoping, wishing, and praying that it was all a dream, someone else's dream.

But it's real. Brett is gone, and I am partly responsible.

My mind is frozen, unable to decide what to do. Where do I go?

I glance at the clock above the fireplace.

It's 7:00 a.m. It's only a matter of time before Cole comes over to torture me again or throw me out.

Guilt is weighing down on me as I climb the stairs. I should have called 911 immediately, even if Brett didn't want me to.

I messed up big time.

I don't make it to the top before the energy drains out of me, and I sink to the steps with my head in my hands. My chest physically aches.

The urge to cry some more is overwhelming, but the tears have dried up again.

Instead, I sit and stare at my surroundings. I so much wanted to call this place home, but it never welcomed me.

When I walked through the front door for the first time, it was like stepping into someone else's life. Now it will never be my home. Now that Brett is gone, Cole might throw us out. But would he do something like that to his own grandson? Is he that cruel?

Yes, he is. He's worse than cruel.

I finally stand again, but before I turn around to head upstairs, the sound of a key turning in the lock of the front door stops me in my tracks.

I clutch my middle as if trying to hold in the pain. Please God, don't let it be Cole. I cannot face him right now.

It's Janella. She looks surprised to see me on the stairs.

I don't even know how to start telling her, or anyone for that matter, what happened to Brett. Maybe I should wait until it comes out in the news. It's only a matter of time. Maybe it already has.

"Sorry, Mrs. Wilton." She clutches the handle of her handbag as she shifts from one foot to the other.

She looks different today. Her braid is not as neat as it usually is, and her eyes are red and puffy. She's even wearing her yellow, knee-length summer dress backwards.

She already knows.

At first, I'm relieved, then I panic because I don't know the exact story being shared by the press. I'm afraid to find out.

I nod and press my lips together. The tears come back to choke me. I allow them to slide down my cheeks unhindered.

"Get sleep." She averts her gaze from mine. "I look after Liam, okay?"

Liam. He will be awake at any moment now. I don't want him to see me crying. Telling him that his father is dead will be the hardest thing I've ever done in my life.

I do need Janella's help. There are a lot of things I will need to take care of, like funeral arrangements. Everything feels so overwhelming that I'm already feeling suffocated before I start.

"Are you sure?" I ask Janella. If she takes care of Liam, I can at least have time alone to grieve.

"Is okay. I do it." Janella twists her hands in front of her. She probably doesn't know how to act around a widow, but she also looks awfully sad. Even though Brett was my husband, she knew him before I did. It's a loss to her as well.

I want to accept her offer, but as much as I want to be alone, I also need to be with Liam, and I want to give Janella a chance to gather herself.

"No. It's okay. I'm taking him out for a bit. You can take the day off if you like. There's not much to do around here."

She nods, but she doesn't turn to leave.

"Janella, is everything all right?"

"I want speak to you, Mrs. Wilton."

I can't imagine anything more important than going to my son right now. She probably wants to hear more about what happened to Brett, and I can't do that, not before I tell Liam his father is dead.

"Can we talk tomorrow?" I ask. "I want to take Liam out for breakfast."

"No. Tomorrow too late. I clean and wait for you." She nods at me and walks in the direction of the kitchen.

Now that Brett is no longer here, maybe she wants to quit her job. Whatever it is she wants to discuss has to wait.

I drag myself like a wet blanket up the rest of the stairs and go to the guest bathroom. I left jeans and a T-shirt in there yesterday morning when I used the shower. I can't bring myself to go into our bedroom. Not yet.

Dressed and ready to go, I make my way to Liam's room.

He opens his eyes as soon as I enter, rubbing them with his fists the way he used to do as a baby.

His curly hair looks shiny in the morning light. I had forgotten to close the blinds last night. I'm surprised the light did not wake him.

"Morning, Superboy." That's what he likes to be called. He told me that one day he will be both a doctor and Superboy.

"Morning, Mommy."

"Liam," I sit down on the edge of his bed, pulling him into my arms, "there's something we need to talk about. But let's go out okay? Let's go and drive around for a bit. Maybe we can have breakfast outside."

Liam loves it when we drive around with no destination in mind. It's something that used to calm him a lot as a baby when he was upset. I hope it will work this time.

"Okay," he says, his eyes brightening. "Is daddy coming too?"

An invisible dagger stabs me in the gut. I

squeeze my eyes to shut out the pain. Then I open them again and shake my head. "No, baby."

"Because he's sleeping," he says.

"Yes." I don't have to tell him now that his father will never wake up again.

I help him get dressed quickly, then we rush downstairs and out the door as he giggles with excitement that breaks my heart.

Our neighbor, Marjorie Smith, is in her garden watering her daisies while her cane leans against the fence that separates our houses. When she sees me, she stops to stare as she always does, but she doesn't wave. She never liked me, and I don't care.

I ignore her and help Liam into the car. The moment we pull out of the driveway, my eye catches sight of a gray Mercedes turning into our street.

My blood boils with hate as I watch his car come into full view.

"It's grandpa." Liam hops up and down in his car seat. "Can he come with us?"

"No, he can't." I tighten my hands on the wheel. "This is our alone time." With that, I step hard on the accelerator, and we drive away in a squeal of tires.

CHAPTER 6

❦

"Should we eat our breakfast in the park?" I ask Liam, trying to be cheerful while dying inside.

I'd planned on taking him to a restaurant for breakfast, but Brett was well-known in our small town. It would be a nightmare if someone came up to me and Liam to offer their condolences before I've even told him. So, we picked up some sandwiches at a small bakery.

The park might be a good idea since, at 8:00 a.m., few or no people will be there. It's also Liam's happy place. I have no idea if it would make a difference, but I want him to be in a comfortable location when I tell him.

"It's early," Liam replies. The delight in his voice is unmistakable.

"It is," I force the words through my throat. "It's nice to do different things, right?"

"Yes, like an adventure. You're the best

mommy in the whole world."

A tear trickles down my cheek. Before today, I believed those words. But I can't today, or ever again. The best mom in the world does not kill her child's father.

The more time I have to mull everything over, the more I believe that I am guilty. My husband wouldn't have died if it weren't for me.

"And you are the best son in the world," I return the compliment because I don't deserve to keep it.

We drive in silence for a while as I try to decide which of the two parks to take Liam to. I'm grateful that my son is not much of a talker.

Both parks in town are deserted, just as I'd hoped. It's no surprise. Who would bring their kids to the park on Thursday morning when they should be at school?

"Did you sleep well last night?" I'm testing the waters, trying to figure out if he saw or heard anything aside from Cole and I arguing.

Liam is a deep sleeper, but between the ambulance and the police, there was a lot of commotion in the house.

"It was fun. There were policemen in my dreams."

My stomach tightens and tears prick the corners of my eyes. "It wasn't a dream," I say in a strained voice. As soon as the words come out, I inhale sharply, wishing I could take them back. I didn't mean to speak them out loud.

Luckily, Liam must not have heard me because he has moved on to another topic.

"Mommy, there's the flower park again," he shouts excitedly, pointing out the window. "I want to go to the flower park."

It's one of the smaller parks and there are brightly colored swings, which Liam loves. Apart from a gray-haired woman taking photos of the roses, no one else is around.

"Okay, let's do it," I say. "Let's go there."

It's hard trying to be brave in front of my son, to be brave not only for him but for both of us. It's something I'll have to do for as long as I live. For the rest of my life, I'll be watching every word I say to him so he doesn't find out the truth about his father's death.

What if one day he wants to know more than I'm prepared to tell him right now? What if we reach a point where he wants to know more? If the truth ever comes out, will he hate me for what I almost did and for lying to him?

"I'm so excited." He laughs and claps his hands. "Is preschool closed?"

Preschool. I forgot about calling in to tell them Liam wouldn't be coming because of a death in the family. I'll have to call them once we're settled in the park. But then again, they probably already know about Brett.

I explain to Liam that preschool is open, but I want to spend the day with him.

The fresh scent of flowers meets us as we exit the car. This time, it does nothing to relax me.

I hold Liam's hand tight as we walk on pebbles until we reach the gate. Like a normal child, he's skipping happily beside me. I hate that I'm about to kill his joy, possibly forever.

The handle of the small gate is cool to the touch even though the summer sun is beating down on us. It opens with a gentle squeak.

Instead of sand, most areas of the park are covered in soft artificial grass to cushion the children's falls. But what about Liam? Once I tell him, will he find a soft place to land?

Liam wants to go the swings immediately, but I tell him to sit with me on one of the red benches first. It's right opposite a beautiful bed of roses.

I pull him onto my lap and hold him tight, pressing my nose into the side of his face, breathing him in. He still smells of the citrus-scented shampoo from his bath yesterday.

"Mommy, you're pressing me too hard." He giggles as he tries to push me away.

"Sorry." I release him, but not completely. I

wish I could hold him forever. I wish I could protect him from the world.

I turn him to face me and place my hands on both sides of his face, unable to control my emotions.

"Why are you crying, Mommy?" He reaches forward and touches my cheek with the tips of his fingers, and the feeling is like butterfly wings against my skin. When he removes them, they're glistening with my tears.

"There's something I need to talk to you about."

"Stop crying, Mommy."

"Mommy is sad." I blink away the tears. "Baby, daddy is gone."

I don't know if I'm doing it right. I have no idea how one explains death to a small child. He knew Brett was very sick. Once Brett was in so much pain during dinner that Liam asked if he will die. Up to that point, I had no idea he knew what death was. I'll never forget the terrified look on his face when he sat there, waiting for our response. Right now, I can't remember what we told him.

"Where did he go?" he asks, playing with the sandwich bag.

"To heaven," I say without hesitation. I have watched several films over the last couple of weeks to try to prepare myself for this moment, but I'm not sure he will be satisfied with my answer.

"He's never coming back?" His eyes lower and his eyelashes brush the top of his cheeks.

I shake my head and lean into him. He doesn't push me away this time. "He's not coming back, baby."

I'm surprised when Liam doesn't ask any more questions. Maybe Brett had prepared him for his death.

"What's going to happen now?" he finally asks. "Will we go and stay with him in heaven?"

I want to smile and cry at the same time. "No, not yet. We still have a lot to do on Earth. Daddy is not here anymore, but we have each other."

"Is daddy's pain gone now?" He pushes back to gaze into my eyes.

"Yes, it is." I thought this would be much harder, but Liam is handling Brett's death so much better than I am.

"Okay. I want to play now." He slides off my lap. He doesn't even shed one tear.

I wish I could get inside his head to see what he's thinking. Has he come to terms with what he heard? Is he trying to escape the conversation because it hurts too much? Maybe it just hasn't sunk in yet.

Liam runs around the park with his arms

outstretched. "I'm an angel," he shouts.

"You *are* an angel," I call back.

He is my angel. If anything is going to hold me together during the next couple of months and years without Brett, it's going to be him.

He occasionally comes back to hug me, especially when he sees me crying, then he goes right back to playing. He's so excited to be at the playground that the sandwiches don't even interest him.

When I call the preschool to let them know that Liam won't be coming, they already know why.

After about forty minutes, I tell him we need to get back to the house. Hopefully, Cole has already left and isn't waiting for us to return. He did call my phone, but I didn't answer. I have nothing to say to him.

What I do know is that I need to get out of his life.

I have no idea where Liam and I will go, but we'll survive.

The envelope.

When Brett asked me to help him die, he told me that there's an envelope in the safe with my name on it. He said if things went wrong, inside it, I'd find everything to help me and Liam escape this toxic environment.

He knew that it might not work, that I might

end up in prison. He knew that euthanasia is a crime in the state of North Carolina. Yet, he begged me to do it anyway. Why would he put me in such a situation?

Whatever the case, I need to go to the house and get the envelope. Then I'll pack our things and check into a hotel with Liam for the next few days. I no longer want to be in a house that belongs to Cole. I don't want him to be a part of our lives under any circumstances.

Once I buckle Liam inside his car seat, I slide behind the wheel. When I drive past the Black Oyster Hotel, the pain inside my chest flares. The hotel towers above most of the buildings in town, majestic and powerful, as intimidating as its owner. I never want to set foot in there again.

I hear the wail of sirens before I see the house. I get close enough to see police cars parked outside and people everywhere.

An ambulance is in front of the house, blocking the street. What happened? Did Cole have a heart attack? His flashy car is parked on the curb.

I want to drive nearer, to find out what happened, but every fiber in my body is telling me to run. The police probably know how Brett died and they came for me.

Before anyone can spot me, I turn the car

around and drive off. I won't give them a chance to arrest me.

The moment the handcuffs click around my wrists, Cole, if he's not hurt, will take my son. He always gets what he wants. But not this time. This is a fight I will never let him win.

CHAPTER 7

～

Cole called my cell phone ten times. Each time, I stared down at the small screen and watched his name flashing across it until it disappeared.

He's the last person I ever want to speak to.

The moment I saw the police in front of the house, I drove to an ATM to withdraw as much money as I could. Once I hit the daily limit, I walked into a bank and asked for a few thousand dollars. When their bank teller asked me to wait, that she needed to discuss something with her manager, I knew that Cole would probably be informed. Money is the only way he can control me now.

As soon as the teller disappeared to the back, I fled the building and drove to a motel.

I'm lying on the bed now, my legs crossed while Liam is watching cartoons. My vision is so blurry that I can barely see what's on the screen.

I'm so tempted to call Robert Kane and come clean about everything that happened, but I know that Cole would never allow him to believe me. How could I trust him or any other police officer in town? Any man who spends his free time with my so-called father-in-law is not one I am willing to trust.

I've read enough books and watched enough movies to know that it's not only the guilty who end up behind bars, but also the innocent. Guilt doesn't matter. All that matters is whether you have a good and expensive lawyer or not, and since I cannot afford one, it would be stupid of me to take the risk.

I'm innocent, but people might not believe me.

Euthanasia is a very controversial topic, and there are many people who believe it's murder. I used to be one of them.

No, the most reasonable thing I can do right now is to lay low.

But where could I hide so Cole can't find us?

When I finally find the courage to listen to Cole's messages, I regret it. Every one of his words drips with poison that sickens me, even though he's not around.

"What the hell do you think you're doing?" he asks from the other end. "Do you really think you can run from the law?"

I glance at the nape of Liam's neck. I watch my little boy pushing his hand into a bag of chips.

What if what I'm doing is wrong? What if it hurts him in the long run?

Then again, I can't imagine hurting him more than Cole could. Even though what I'm doing will make me look even more guilty to a lot of people, I need to do this.

"You can run, but I will find you," Cole continues. "And trust me, I will make you suffer before I hand you over to the police. You are a murderer and you will pay. You hear me?"

I switch off the phone. I can't bear to hear more. It hurts too much. I don't know whether I'll ever have the courage to switch it on again.

I need to leave town. There's no reason for me to stay. My father-in-law is a psychopath, and I don't really have friends. The only friends I used to have were my colleagues at the hotel, but as soon as I married Brett, they all pulled away from me. When I tried to reach out to them, especially to Denise Sanchez, who I really liked, Brett discouraged me from speaking to "the help." I knew then that it was not his decision, but his father's.

I tried to make friends with the people in his circle, but even though they never said it, they all believed that I married Brett for his money. They secretly despised me. They never thought a woman who didn't come from money deserved to be his wife. So, I was alone for most of my marriage with Brett.

But that wasn't new to me. I have been a loner since my childhood. I know how to retreat to a deep place inside of me, to hide from the world.

When Liam was born, he became my best friend. I had always wanted my husband to be my best friend. I consider a friend to be someone you can tell all your deep and dark secrets. Brett was never that person, and now he never could be.

Now my relationship with Liam is threatened by the secret I will have to keep from him forever.

I wish I could go back to the house to get the envelope Brett left behind. From the way he said it, I suspected there would be some passports and maybe money to help me and Liam start over. But going back there is too much of a risk. I'm pretty sure the cops are watching the house. Cole is probably there waiting for me.

I feel stuck, terrified, and empty.

Growing up as an orphan, I thought I knew what loneliness was. I thought I knew what emptiness was, but as it turns out, I had no idea. This is true loneliness, and coupled with fear, it's starting to suffocate me.

I don't like it when Liam watches too much TV. I want him to play games and read books, but right now I've never been more grateful for television. As long as his eyes are fixed on the screen, we don't have to speak.

I never thought there would come a day when I didn't want to speak to my son. I'm terrified of the questions he will ask, dreading the look in his eyes as he searches mine for answers and the truth.

I don't want to have to lie to him about what really happened to his father. One day he will ask, but until then, I will have enough time to get my story straight.

I curl into a fetal position, hugging my middle with both my arms.

I'm not a criminal. I don't know what criminals do in these situations. I don't know how one goes about trying to disappear. I don't even know whether I can disappear without being caught. For all I know, the police are guarding the entrance to Fort Haven, checking each car that comes and goes.

I can't think. I'm too exhausted by trying to keep myself sane. My anxiety is at its peak right now, and I don't even have my medication.

I do the only thing I have the power to do. I sleep. I need to stay awake, to keep watch, but my eyes are closing involuntarily. Maybe sleep will help clear my head, so I can come up with a plan.

*

I don't know how long I've been sleeping, but the sound of the TV blaring wakes me up again. For a moment, I think Liam has fallen asleep next to me, but he's awake and still eating his chips. Since I never let him watch that much TV, he's making the most of it.

As soon as I move, Liam looks at me excitedly. "Mommy," he points at the TV screen, "Janella is on TV. Look at her picture."

Liam is right. He has changed the channel. Instead of the cartoon channel, he's watching the news. My eyes widen with shock as I try to focus on the TV screen. My heart jumps to my throat and I sit up. It takes a moment for me to take in what's in front of me.

The headline that scrolls across the screen causes blood to rush to my head.

Meghan Wilton wanted for the murder of her husband and housekeeper.

Swallowing down the bile that's pushing its way up my throat, I act fast. It's only a matter of time before they show my picture.

I grab the remote from Liam and switch off

the TV.

"No!" Liam shouts, trying to take back the remote. "They said your name. You're famous. Let's watch."

I can't respond to him. I'm still trying to digest what I read.

What the hell is going on?

"I'll be... I'll be right back." I get to my feet and charge into the small bathroom, still clutching the remote. I'm afraid he might switch the TV back on.

Once I lock the door, I drop to the floor. Janella is dead? And I'm wanted for murder?

I expected that they would think I killed Brett, especially since I'm clearly running. But Janella?

I cover my mouth with my hands. My pulse is racing. It was Cole. He did it.

When I left the house, Janella was still alive, and he was just arriving. If she's dead, he has something to do with it. But why would he kill her?

I know the answer. He wants to punish me. He wants to make sure I go to prison for life. I know what kind of man he is, the depth of his evil, and how dangerous he is, but I never thought he was a murderer. He belongs behind bars.

Is it time for me to tell the police what I

know about him? Would it be enough to send him to prison?

No. I can never talk to the cops without ending up behind bars as well.

How could I ever prove that I'm innocent of two murders, especially after disappearing for almost a full day? Trembling, I rise to my feet and splash my face with cold water. I don't bother to wipe it away so it drips down onto my T-shirt.

It's over. My whole life has crashed and burned.

I lower myself onto the toilet.

Pressing my head between my legs, I force myself to breathe.

From a distance, Liam calls my name, but I don't answer.

I don't feel the vomit gushing out of my mouth, I only notice when it flows down my legs and pools at my feet.

"Mommy, open the door," Liam begs from the other side.

I wipe my mouth with the back of my hand and force myself to get up. "I'm coming," I say, my voice shaking.

I wish I was alone and could allow grief to break me apart without it terrifying my son. But I can't. I can't stay frozen for long. I need to force myself to function.

I wash my face again and rinse my mouth, then I use one of the towels in the bathroom to wipe away the vomit before rinsing it as well.

When I opened the door again, Liam is standing there. He's all I have left.

"Are you okay, Mommy?" He gazes up into my face, frowning a little.

It hurts to smile, but I try. "I was a bit sad."

He gathers me into his arms. "Don't cry. Daddy is sleeping in heaven."

More tears come, falling onto his little head. I hold him until he pushes away again.

I drop to my feet and hold his hands in mine. "You and Mommy are going on a great adventure."

"Are we going camping?" he asks.

Liam loves everything that has to do with the outdoors. The one time we went camping, he had the time of his life.

"No, not camping, but we're going far away. We will have so much fun together." Fun is not a word I'll ever use to describe my life again.

"I'm in." He raises his little hand for a high-five. As my palm meets his, I promise to never let him down. I promise silently to never let him get hurt, even if I get hurt in the process.

PART TWO

CHAPTER 8
One year later

～⌒～

Willow Creek, a small town of only three thousand residents, is located in Tennessee and a little over three hours from Fort Haven.

The residents of Willow Creek remain in the dark when it comes to my true identity. I prefer to keep it that way. They think of me as the crazy widow who lives in an old cabin in the woods with her son, Clark. I *am* a widow, but I'm far from being crazy.

Or am I?

Maybe it's a good thing. Being eccentric keeps them away from us.

My new name is Zoe Roberts, but not many people call me that. "Crazy Lady" is more interesting, I guess. Fine by me.

Liam chose the name Clark for himself, like his favorite superhero. I told him we were spies and needed new names to stay undercover.

After using Clark for a while, he got used to it, and I got used to even calling him by his new name in my dreams. It both relieved and broke my heart.

Mrs. Ruth Foster is one of the few people who see me as a normal person, and she's my lifesaver.

"You go and have yourself a good day," she says with a bright smile as she reaches for Clark's hand. "I'll take good care of your little man."

"I know you will." My lips stretch into a smile, a small gift for the woman who has given us shelter for nine months. The old cabin we call home belongs to her, and she takes care of my son when I go to work. She even homeschools him, as she used to be a teacher.

She doesn't know who I am either, but she's not the curious type. Nine months ago, when she caught us squatting in her abandoned cabin, all she needed to hear was that we had nowhere to go and we needed shelter for a few days. In exchange, she asked me to pay very little rent. Days morphed into weeks and weeks into months.

My little boy stole the fifty-eight-year-old woman's heart, and she gave us permission to stay for as long as we liked. She laughed when she told me that the cabin had once belonged to her late husband, Jacob, who escaped to it a few times a week to get away from her nagging.

When Mrs. Foster offered to care for Clark when I worked, I was hesitant at first, but she insisted, and I did need her help. As a young woman, she had founded the first kindergarten in town, and she said that seeing kids every day lit up her life. In a way, I feel like Clark may be safer with her than with me.

"I'll pick him up at eight." I ruffle Clark's hair.

One thing I've learned while being on the run is that I need to keep every single one of my promises. The last thing I need is to get on someone's bad side. I do what I promise to do, and I try my best to be where I say I'll be at the agreed-upon time.

Rocking the boat is not part of the plan.

I step away from the door and wave at both of them as I walk to my used Chevy hatchback. Behind the wheel, I draw in a shaky breath.

It's been a year, and I have not been found, but it doesn't get any easier. Every day I keep waiting for the other shoe to drop, for the cops to arrest me or for Cole to show up.

Even though I try not to think about him, I can never forget his last words to me.

You can run, but I will find you.

I don't doubt for a second that if he finds

me, he will punish me for the crimes he thinks I committed.

As soon as I saw on the news that I was wanted for murdering two people, I abandoned our car at the motel, took my son and the little money we had, and got on a bus out of town. Before moving to Willow Creek, we hid out in several towns across Florida, never staying in one place for longer than a week.

Mrs. Foster is at the window now, so I drive away before she wonders why I'm not leaving.

Finding a job as a newcomer in a close-knit town was tough, but Mrs. Foster helped get me a waitressing job at the Lemon Cafe' & Restaurant, which belongs to her acquaintance, Tasha Lake.

As I drive through town, I focus on my destination. I go where I'm going and come back when I say I will. I don't go to visit unnecessary places. I go to work, I buy groceries, and I take care of important chores.

Like the fruit it's named after, the Lemon (or just Lemon, as the locals call it) has a bright yellow exterior and round tables with striped yellow and white tablecloths. Even the air inside is lemon-scented. In case it wasn't obvious, lemons are Tasha's favorite fruit.

When I walk into the restaurant, there are

only a handful of regulars occupying the tables. They glance at me briefly before returning to the pork chops and potato salad lunch special, along with the signature fresh mint lemonade that's always on the menu.

A part of me is always expecting to find Cole sitting at one of the tables.

I only have a short discussion with Tasha, the owner, before getting to work. I always aim to do more than what is expected of me.

The days are long and it's one of the hottest days this year so far. There isn't even much of a breeze coming through the open windows.

The lunch special displayed on the chalkboard outside the restaurant draws in more people than usual. Normally, it's my cue to help out in the kitchen for a while.

Two months ago, Raphael, the head chef, suffered a terrible migraine and had to leave work early. Since there was no one to replace him, and the guests were demanding their food, I asked to step in. My cooking skills impressed everyone to the point that I now work with one foot in the kitchen and the other in the dining room. I prefer it that way. When my anxiety takes over and I become paranoid about Cole walking in, I can retreat to the kitchen.

But not today. Today we only have three

waitstaff instead of the usual four and the kitchen is fully staffed.

"You are a godsend, you know that?" Tasha comes to stand next to me as the lunch guests start trickling out, and we have a moment to catch our breaths.

"What do you mean?" I wipe the sweat off my brow with a napkin.

"You seriously don't know what I'm talking about?" She raises an eyebrow.

Tasha is a year younger than me, with dark brown skin and dark hair in twists that are always piled up in a messy bun on top of her head when she's working. In her long, flowing skirts, melon-colored tops, and the lemon earrings she is so fond of, she fits right into the feel of her restaurant.

The Lemon is Tasha's pride and joy that she built from the ground up. Before I came along, she apparently ran it with her brother until he left to open up his own club. According to her, his new place attracts a lot of locals and visitors, but I wouldn't know. I don't visit bars or clubs.

"I really don't know what you're talking about, Tasha." I grab a rag to go and wipe down the table of the last guests to leave.

She follows me, arranging the chairs while I wipe away crumbs and gravy.

"You are a really hard worker. Do you ever take a moment to breathe?"

Breathe? I have forgotten how to do that, especially since I tread water every day. But, of course, she doesn't know that.

"I love working. You pay me to do it." My pay is not much, but it's enough to pay the rent and buy groceries. I always put the tips in a savings jar at home for rainy days. "I'm grateful for this job."

"Tasha, Zoe, see you tomorrow."

We both turn to wave at Sandy, one of the other waitresses. She studies at the University of Tennessee in Knoxville and works at Lemon when she comes home for the weekends.

"I guess I'm telling you that I appreciate having you as an employee. Sometimes, I wonder what we would do without you."

"What you did before me." I give her a smile.

"Trust me, before you came along, we could barely hold our heads above water." She touches my arm. "You really do a lot here, but I want you to take some time off to get some rest and spend time with your son."

"I do take the weekends off."

"I know, but you still come in sometimes when we're short-staffed."

"I love working here." I don't tell her that

working hard keeps me from thinking too much and every tip I get from a customer makes a difference.

"That makes me happy to hear." Tasha squeezes my arm. "But if you ever need a couple of days off, let me know. I already feel guilty as it is. As your boss, I insist that you take a short break now before the dinner guests arrive." She stretches out her hand for the rag. "We could have coffee together if you like."

"Yeah, that would be nice."

She wants us to be friends. She always takes time out of her day to chat with me, and three times she invited me and Clark to her house to have dinner with her, her husband, and their twin boys. I always decline. Being a recluse is safer for me. I only get out of the cabin when I absolutely have to. Socializing is not a necessity.

But an occasional coffee with Tasha at the restaurant when things are slow is appreciated. But it's also exhausting because it takes a lot of effort to filter every word I say, so I don't blow my cover.

The news of Brett's and Janella's murders was so big that it reached Willow Creek. Not long after I arrived, my old face was still in the newspapers with the word "wanted" in the headlines. Now things have died down, but I still need to keep my guard up.

*

After our short break, a man with black jeans and a leather jacket struts in, and we stop what we're doing and stare. He has a square face, a well-formed nose, full lips, and perfectly shaped eyebrows above moss green eyes.

We're not the only ones staring at him. Eva, the youngest waitress, is practically drooling. She was watering the plant near the restaurant entrance, but now the water can is neglected at her feet and her mouth is wide open.

Tasha leans into me and whispers. "If I weren't married to my dream man, I'd gladly commit a crime just so he can arrest me."

"He's a police officer?" I instantly snap back to reality.

"Brand spanking new in town. He's probably off-duty, hence the lack of uniform. Apparently, he's been working for the WCPD for a week or two now, but it's his first time dropping by." She gives me a small shove. "You should go and get his order."

"I... no." My pulse is starting to race. "I was going to ask Raphael if he needs a hand with dinner preparations."

"No need. He has everything under control. I checked with him. Now go and help the gentleman. We need to make a good impression. That's why I'm sending him my best employee. Make him feel very welcome." Tasha winks. "I have some paperwork to do in the office. Call me when more guests start arriving."

I swallow hard. "Okay."

She's my boss. I have to do what she asks, even if I'd rather run.

With trembling hands, I take my notebook and a pen, push back my shoulders, and head to his table. He's already flipping through the menu.

When I arrive at the table, he looks up with a smile. "Hey there."

"Hi, welcome to Lemon," I say, my pen hovering over my notebook. "What can I get you?"

"How about a big glass of vodka?" His eyes crinkle at the corners as he grins.

"I... sorry, umm, we don't have vodka. Is there anything else I can offer you?"

"I'm kidding." He chuckles. "I'm about to start my shift, so no alcohol for me."

"Okay." I do feel slight relief that he hasn't come to arrest me, unless he's just getting ready to pounce and handcuff me by surprise.

"Let me see." He lowers his gaze to the laminated menu and takes his time choosing something else.

"Please bring me a fish burger with lots of hot sauce and a large Coke."

"Of course. I'll be right back with your drink...first."

I can feel his gaze following me to the front of the restaurant. What is he thinking? Is he wondering why I look so nervous? Does it show from the outside?

When I return to his table, his drink is chilling my palm and my knees are so wobbly with fear I can barely walk.

"I haven't seen you around." He lifts the drink to his lips. "It's been interesting getting to know the locals. I've only been in Willow Creek for two weeks. So, what's your name?" he asks.

"Zoe," I murmur.

"Zoe," he repeats. "It's a pleasure to meet you, Zoe." He stretches out his hand.

I glance past him and notice Tasha watching us from the kitchen entrance. She's clearly pleased.

"Nice to meet you." I shake his hand quickly.

"I'm Officer Tim Roland, but you can call me Tim."

"Okay." I don't want to call him anything at all. I want to serve him his food and then hopefully never speak to him again.

"I'll bring your meal." I turn on my heel. My knees are threatening to give away.

Tasha hurries to me. "Is he as good-looking close up? I think he likes you. He actually has his eyes on you right now."

"It doesn't matter. I'm not interested."

"But you said your husband has been dead for over a year now. You still don't want to date?"

"I'm not ready." I swallow hard.

Tasha tries to get me to open up some more, but I don't lower the wall between us.

She gives up and we have to return to work because more guests have arrived. I throw myself into the dinner service, glad for the distraction.

I don't speak to Officer Roland again until he leaves, giving me a tip larger than the amount he spent on his food. I tried to give some of the money back, but he refused.

I hope he won't come again during my shift.

At the end of my shift, I drive to Mrs. Foster's to pick up Clark. My heart almost breaks inside my chest when I don't find them at the house. She's not answering her phone, either.

I drive around town frantically, afraid that Cole found us and has taken Clark.

I'm close to going crazy with worry when

Mrs. Foster returns my call. They're back at the house.

When I get there, Clark runs into my arms. "Hello, Mommy."

I'm still shaking as I pull him close.

"Good evening, Zoe," Mrs. Foster says. "Clark was such a good boy that I promised him ice cream after dinner."

I shut my eyes, trying hard to control my emotions. I can't lash out at Mrs. Foster. I need her, and in a normal world, she did nothing wrong. She cares about my son and wanted to give him a treat.

"Thank you," I say through my dry throat. "But next time, please let me know if you want to take Clark out."

"I didn't think you would mind."

"I... I don't want to worry, that's all."

She clasps her hands in front of her. "Okay. I understand. It won't happen again and certainly not this late."

I nod and force a smile. "Thank you again for your help."

The fear of losing my son almost killed me. Hopefully, my worst nightmare will never come true.

CHAPTER 9

Cole is standing in front of me, the end of his cigar glowing at the tip, the smoke rising to mask his features.

He's watching me tied to a chair, unable to move. The chains around my wrists and ankles cut into my skin.

He pulls on his cigar again, then takes one step toward me.

"Try to run now," he says menacingly. "You can never outrun me. I'll be right behind you."

He blows the next puff of smoke into my face. I choke on it, my lungs rejecting the foreign particles.

Cole grabs me by the throat, cutting off my air supply. I gasp for air, but he doesn't loosen his grip. It's only when my head starts to spin from lack of oxygen that he steps back and reaches into his pocket.

He removes a lighter and flicks it on.

My eyes widen and my insides curl with fear.

I want to beg him to let me go, but I can't speak. My mouth is not covered, but fear kills the words before they can surface.

I push my feet against the floor, trying to slide away from him. The soles of my feet slide against something wet. A toxic smell engulfs me, so strong that it burns my nostrils.

He wants to set me on fire.

I start to kick and force myself to scream.

He doesn't care. He tosses the lighter at the floor and it meets the alcohol in a burst of flames that lick their way to me.

When the fire reaches my skin, my screams finally erupt. I scream and cry until a soft touch on my cheek makes me open my eyes.

I sag deeper into the mattress with relief when it hits me that I was dreaming. Cole is not here.

"Wake up, Mommy," Clark calls, touching my sweaty cheek again.

We sleep in the same bed because I never want to be apart from him. I don't want to wake up one day to find him gone.

"Mommy, you were crying again in your sleep." His voice is still sleepy. I woke him with my struggling.

"I'm so sorry, baby." I wipe the sweat from my forehead and pull him into my arms. "I had a bad dream."

"Don't be scared. It's not real."

I bury my head into his little body, wishing he could protect me from my inner demons. I used to have nightmares at least once a week, but the past few days they have been happening almost every night. I hate that I scare Clark with my night terrors.

After I release him, I take my anxiety medication to calm me down.

It's already 7:00 a.m. on Saturday and I have the day free.

"Go brush your teeth. After my shower, we can bake. How about cupcakes for Mrs. Foster?"

I still feel guilty about being angry with her two days ago when she took Clark out for ice cream.

In addition to my new hobby of extreme couponing, baking calms me down. Growing up at a group home in New Jersey, my main task used to be helping out in the kitchen. At first, I hated it, but then Virginia, the cook, taught me how to love cooking and baking. It soon became my escape. It still is.

When I create a beautiful sweet treat, I convince myself that I'm not as useless as I think I am. Even a broken person is capable of creating something beautiful.

Creating something from nothing gives me

a sense of purpose, but the good feelings only last until the oven is switched off, the flour is wiped off the counter, and the baking tools are put away.

Clark loves to watch me bake and I love that at that moment, his little mind is focused on something more beautiful than the dark memories of his father's death. He doesn't talk about it, but he can't have left Fort Haven unscathed.

"What kind of cupcakes should we bake?" I ask him after my shower.

"Mrs. Foster likes chocolate. You know that, Mommy."

"You're right. Sorry, I forgot."

We go to the kitchen hand in hand, where I disappear into the tiny pantry. I gather everything I need and get out before I become claustrophobic. Some people might find my fear of being trapped inside small spaces ridiculous, but it's a fear I'd had since I was a child and haven't managed to shake off. That's why I keep the ingredients we need most of the time inside the kitchen cabinets.

Ten minutes later, the kitchen is transformed into our own personal bakery.

It's strange that even though I'm a baker, I don't have much of a sweet tooth. I taste what I bake only to see if I'm headed in the right direction, but I never enjoy the final product. I just bake for other people, who happen to be Clark and Mrs. Foster at the moment. Sometimes I bake at Lemon, but usually, Tasha purchases her baked goods from Jody Sweet, a local bakery.

When I pour the flour into a bowl, flower dust floats upward into my face.

Clark laughs. For a split second, I allow myself to join him. I don't know what horrors today will bring, but this moment is ours alone. We don't get to go out much, but we get to do this.

The red and white '50s diner-style kitchen with its checkerboard floors and vintage-inspired backsplashes makes me feel like I can escape to another time and place and pretend my problems don't exist.

Clark helps me stir the cupcake mixture and fill the baking tray. Once the cupcakes are in the oven and I'm cleaning up, he gets his coloring book to make the time go faster.

When the cupcakes are done, and the aromas of chocolate, lemon zest, and vanilla swirl around the room, he helps me decorate them with buttercream, lemon slices, and mint leaves.

Now that we've finished baking, dread wraps itself around me. I can't help feeling that something bad is about to happen. It's the same feeling I had the night Brett died, seconds before I found him in our room.

But I pretend for Clark that I'm in a good mood, and we grab the cupcakes and drive them to Mrs. Foster to surprise her.

We find her sitting out on the porch, knitting something that looks like a scarf. She says it's for Clark and puts it away quickly.

I'm touched, but I wonder if Clark will ever wear it. Will we still be in Willow Creek when winter comes around?

"Is that for me?" Mrs. Foster asks, pointing at the tray in Clark's hands.

"They're cupcakes!" Clark says before I can answer.

"You really like to surprise me, don't you, Clark?" She smiles brightly.

"I helped Mommy bake them."

"You are one talented boy." Mrs. Foster takes one of the cupcakes from the tray. She brings it to her lips and bites into it. "Delicious as usual." She raises her gaze to mine. "Have you thought more about what I said?" she asks, chewing.

She has been telling me often to open up my own bakery or restaurant. I'm always flattered that she thinks my baked goods are good enough to charge for.

"Yes." I pull my gaze from hers. If only she knew how complicated it is. I can never tell her what's standing in the way of my dream. "Maybe someday I will."

I simply smile, hoping she will drop the topic. I'm relieved when she goes back to chatting with Clark, telling him stories of her childhood, as if he were her own grandchild.

"Unfortunately, we have to go," I say after the third story.

"Why don't you leave Clark with me? He can keep me company."

"I'd love to, but I promised him another ice cream because he was so good in the kitchen today." That's not the whole truth. Mostly, I want to spend time with my son instead of handing him over.

"Well, in that case, off you go, young man." Mrs. Foster ruffles Clark's hair and he slides down off the porch swing.

When we get back into the car, she gives us a small wave and returns to her knitting, the tray of cupcakes next to her.

Although Clark would have loved to sit at an ice cream shop, I can't risk being out in public for too long. That's why we never eat at restaurants, except occasionally when he comes with me to work on days when Mrs. Foster is unable to babysit.

Instead, we drive to the grocery store to pick up a tub of ice cream.

I'm about to pay when my body senses a strong presence behind me, a tingling sensation as if I'm being watched.

I spin around and scan the faces behind me, but there are none that I recognize, and no one comes across as suspicious.

Still feeling uneasy, I pay for the ice cream and grab Clark's hand.

What if *he* had been watching me and stepped out of sight when I turned around? What if the reason I'm having so many nightmares is that he's getting close?

What if Cole is in town?

But then, why didn't he come sooner? What stopped him from hiring a detective to track me down? It's been a year and he hasn't managed to do it.

Maybe he wants to punish me from a distance.

Inside the car, Clark wants to start eating the ice cream right away. I tell him he can't because he doesn't have a spoon. He insists on using his finger. Usually, I stand my ground, but I don't have the energy to right now.

I give him the tub of ice cream and he digs into it, licking his fingers with glee.

Once we get to the cabin, my stomach is in

knots. As always, I tour the entire cabin, making sure everything is in its place.

Inside the kitchen, a cold shower of dread washes over me when I notice that one of the three cupcakes, we left behind is missing. I had meant for Clark to eat them for dessert tonight.

I call Clark and he comes running.

"Did you eat one of the cupcakes?" I ask him, trying not to think the worst.

"No." He shakes his head.

"I left three cupcakes for you to eat for dessert, remember?"

He eyes the cupcakes on the table and shakes his head again. "No, Mommy, I think you only left two."

He can't be right. I'm pretty sure I left three cupcakes.

"Sweetie," I say, turning him to face me, "did you just forget? It's okay to tell mommy if you don't remember."

"I didn't forget." He stomps one of his feet. "I'm not lying, mommy. I'm not."

"Of course not, baby. Of course not." Feeling terrible, I pull him to me and kiss the top of his head.

A moment later, he leaves me standing in the kitchen, wondering whether I'm finally losing my mind.

CHAPTER 10

As soon as Clark falls asleep, I put away the book I was reading to him and tiptoe out of the room, closing the door softly.

The online newspaper articles I printed out at the restaurant today are sitting in the living room.

I don't own a laptop, so Tasha gave me permission to use the computer in her office whenever I want, but I'm always nervous that I might leave behind some clues about who I am. I only use it once a month and always make sure to delete my history after I'm done.

I can barely breathe as I spread out the articles related to Brett's and Janella's murders.

Two days later, I'm still haunted by the missing cupcake, still wondering if I was being paranoid or if someone was inside the cabin.

I asked Clark several times more if he is sure that there were only two cupcakes. The answer was always yes.

I want to believe him, but something won't let me.

I brace myself and pick up the first article. It's an old article I already read not long after I left Fort Haven. I put it down again and sift through the papers to find a more recent one that would give me more accurate information about how close the law is to catching up with me.

I find one that's only two days old, and my breath catches in my throat.

They haven't given up. They're still searching for me.

Photos of me grace the page. My fingers stroke the birthmark on my collarbone. When changing my looks, it's the one thing I cannot change, but I keep it well hidden underneath clothing and makeup.

My breath is shaking as it goes in and out of my lungs. Each word I take in feels like a dagger to my heart.

The new police chief of Fort Haven has vowed to find Brett Wilton's murderer. Apparently, the previous chief of police died in a car accident two months ago.

I scan the article, but I am not able to read every word, only the sentences that spring out at me.

Meghan Wilton is wanted for the murder of her husband, Brett Wilton, and their housekeeper. Cole Wilton, Brett Wilton's father, is offering a reward of $20,000 to anyone who informs him of his former daughter-in-law's whereabouts. He refuses to give up hope that she will be found and brought to justice and he can be reunited with his only grandson.

The tragedy of Brett Wilton's death had shaken the small town of Fort Haven. He was found dead in his home on June 20 last year. Only hours later, the housekeeper, Janella Soriano was also found dead, poisoned to death with cyanide, the same poison that is believed to have killed Brett Wilton. After being initially questioned by police, Meghan Wilton disappeared from Fort Haven with her son and was never seen again.

If you or anyone you know has any information pertaining to her whereabouts, we urge you to contact the police or Cole Wilton as soon as possible.

The piece of paper flutters to the carpet. My gaze follows it. It's the first time I'm hearing what killed my husband. How he died does not matter anymore. What matters is that I'm still wanted by the police.

I thought the case was running cold, that they had given up on me. But then again, a year is not a long time, especially when it comes to murder. And I never really expected Cole to give up. He's not that kind of man.

I've managed to hide for a year, but it feels as though I'm reaching the end. Now that there is a reward on my head, people will be more motivated to search for me. Someone here in Willow Creek might recognize me and notify the cops.

I don't understand why they're asked to contact Cole as well. Why not just the police?

My mouth goes sour. Cole would prefer them to contact him so he can get to me first. He would want to have enough time to torture me before handing me over. I'm also guessing that if someone is greedy, they would contact him first in order to negotiate a higher amount.

I stare at the piece of paper at my feet into the eyes of the man I used to call my father-in-law. There's a small photo of him along with one of Brett. The confidence in Cole's eyes makes me want to throw up.

Without thinking, I snatch up the page and tear it to shreds.

I want to cry so much, to scream out, but I don't want Clark to hear me. I rush out onto the porch, my fingers pressed hard against my throbbing temples, my teeth grinding against each other as I replay every word I read in my mind.

What do I do? Do I run again? And if I do, where would I go? I feel safer in the cabin that has protected me for several months now. The thought of starting over in another town without anyone's help terrifies me.

I force myself to calm down, filling my lungs with as much air as possible. I need to think. I cannot allow myself to come apart. I have Clark to think about.

There's only one thing for me to do right now. I need to lay low for a few days. I need to stay out of the public eye. Being seen anywhere right now is dangerous.

I lower myself onto the porch swing and put my head into my hands only for a moment before it snaps up again. I don't know if it's my paranoia, but I feel as though I'm being watched.

I search the darkness and find nothing. The only thing I can make out are the sounds of small animals skittering in the underbrush. Still, I go back into the cabin and lock the door. I also make sure every single window is closed.

Then, I go to the bathroom and open the cabinet, removing one of the hair color boxes stacked inside. Blonde is my next look.

When I left Fort Haven, I was a long-haired brunette. Now I aim to have a different look every few weeks. Sometimes I cut my hair shorter or allow it to grow longer. I alternate between the two.

It's important I don't look the same for too long. I also wear various shades of contact lenses to disguise my amber eyes. Changing up my look when my gut tells me to, makes me feel safer, less recognizable. But on the other hand, it has caused Tasha to ask questions. I told her I get bored and like shaking things up a bit.

People at work, except for Tasha, have started to guess what color of hair I'll have next. They haven't said it in front of me, but I've heard the whispers.

I've become such an expert at coloring my hair that it doesn't take long. Finally, I'm standing in front of the small round mirror, studying my new look. The blonde hair makes me look pale and washed out, but I don't care. Deep down, I know that I still look like myself. Can I truly ever look different? Or do I only feel this way because I know myself better than anyone else?

An untrained eye might not recognize that the woman whose photo is displayed in the articles is the same one who walks the streets of Willow Creek.

The colors I choose for my hair and my eyes aren't flashy. Right now, I'm choosing velvet brown for my eyes.

When I return from the bathroom, smelling of ammonia from hair dye, I can barely walk with exhaustion, both physical and mental.

As soon as I enter, Clark coughs and I freeze in the doorway. I hold my breath, expecting him to go back to sleep after stretching out a bit, but he doesn't. Instead, he sits up in the dark and calls my name.

Kicking myself for being too loud, I head over to the bed and switch on the nightlight on my side.

"Sweetie, why are you not sleeping?"

"I heard sounds." He rubs his eyes with his fists.

"What sounds?" I frown and glance frantically at the window.

He shrugs. "I don't know." Sleep disappears from his eyes the longer he looks at me. "Mommy, you did it again."

I bring my hand to my hair. "You don't like it?"

He shakes his head. "I liked the other one, the red hair."

I sigh with disappointment. Sometimes Clark likes my looks and sometimes he doesn't. I do hate that when he starts getting used to the way I look, I change myself again. It has to make him feel insecure.

But there's nothing I can do. I need to keep running.

The next few days will be critical. We will be more careful than we have ever been before.

I pray that no one will recognize us. The good thing about Clark is that he has changed so much in the past year. He looked so small in the photos that were originally circulated on the news and by the police.

No matter what, I would never change my son's hair or eye color. I don't want him to develop a complex, to think that I don't love him the way he is and feel the need to change him. But sometimes I give him disguises like sunglasses, reminding him that we are undercover.

"Can you have red hair again next time?" he asks innocently.

"Maybe, but you need to go to bed, Superboy. Should I read you another story?"

"No, Mommy." He draws closer to me on the bed. "Can you make up one?"

I don't know how I will be able to make up a story with my head filled with fear. But to my surprise, I manage. By the time I'm done, Clark is sleeping again.

I switch off the light, but I can't sleep. I continue to search the darkness for all the dangers hiding there.

My ears are so trained to listen to every sound that I catch that of a dog barking from a distance, and the river that runs past the cabin.

The loudest sound is that of my heart thudding inside my chest.

I lie down on my pillow and try to make sense of everything that happened. After all this time, I still don't understand why Cole would kill Janella.

Something from the article slips into my mind and makes me sit up again. They said Janella was killed with the same poison that is suspected to have killed Brett.

My eyes grow wide. What if it was him? What if it was Cole who killed Brett? I don't know how he could've done it, but the fact that Janella was killed with the same poison that killed him means that they were murdered by the same person.

Janella wanted to speak to me that day. I can't help feeling that if I had taken the time to listen, she would still be alive.

Something else hits me. Brett promised me that the medication that would kill him would be undetectable. He didn't want to get me into trouble. And yet, they found it.

After running it over in my head, I now believe without a doubt that Brett did not kill himself. Whoever injected the poison into his veins must have come with another poison and used both on him.

He was too weak and in too much pain to pick up the syringe from the floor and inject the poison into his veins.

Plus, I was away for no longer than fifteen minutes. I know from experience that when pain struck him and he refused to take painkillers, it lasted at least half an hour, if not longer. On the night of his death he didn't have an ounce of strength in him, and he couldn't have regained it in the short time that I was out of the room.

It was Cole. But I can't prove it. I can't go to the cops and risk being the one behind bars. Cole is a powerful man and I'm pretty sure he engineered evidence to prove that I am guilty. He also had such close relationships to the local officials and law enforcement that I wouldn't have a chance. He would probably pay them all off to put me in jail forever, or worse.

Maybe if I didn't have Clark, I would try, but if I take this risk and fail, Cole will take my son. I need to protect Clark. For a few days, I need to keep him close to me. If Cole ever finds us, I don't know what he will do.

CHAPTER 11

My heart sinks as I listen to Tasha on the other side of the line.

"I'm sorry, Zoe. I know I said you should take some days off if you need to, but it's not a good time right now. I really need you for the next two days. Sandy is going to a funeral out of town and we have two birthday parties. We might also need you in the kitchen."

I sent her a text message last night before I fell asleep, telling her I needed the next two days off. She did not respond until this morning.

"Zoe, are you there? Is everything all right?"

"Yes." I glance at Clark, who is playing with Legos on the kitchen table. Mrs. Foster bought them for him. "I'm not feeling well. I was hoping you could manage without me."

"I'm really sorry. I want to give you today and tomorrow off, but there's so much going on. I promise you that after things calm down, you can take a couple weeks."

I have two options. I can refuse to go to work and possibly lose my job, or I can go and hope nobody recognizes me. Even though I look completely different from the woman I used to be, my paranoia will continue to taunt me.

"I don't know." I watch the clock on the wall. I want to help Tasha, but I'm terrified of stepping out of the cabin.

"How about you come for only two or three hours today? Please, Zoe. I need you. We are really short-staffed."

I squeeze my eyes shut and tighten my hand around the phone. Tasha has always been good to me and I feel terrible for even thinking of letting her down. And I need the money, especially the tips.

Maybe it will be fine. The chances of anyone recognizing me are slim.

"Okay." I blow out a breath. "I can do that. I'll be there within the hour."

"Thank you so much," Tasha says, and we hang up.

The next person I call is Mrs. Foster.

I called her a few minutes ago to let her know I have the day off and will be spending my free time with Clark. She had sounded disappointed because she's so used to seeing him almost every day during the week. When I now tell her that my plans have changed and he will be going to her, after all, she's unable to hide her delight.

After I hang up the phone, I tell Clark that I need to work. His little face crumples.

"But you promised to stay with me today. We were going to make cookies."

"I'm sorry, baby, but Tasha needs me to come in. And you always have so much fun with Mrs. Foster. I'm sure she'll be very happy to see you."

Clark only shrugs as I get him ready.

"You need to make it up to me," he says on the way to drop him off. It's amazing how kids use the words they hear us repeating often. I don't know how many times I have told him that I will make it up to him, how many times I've disappointed him.

"Yes." I'm relieved he's talking to me again. "How should I do that?"

"Ice cream," he says and I shake my head.

"You had too much ice cream the past few days."

"But Mommy, you owe me." I want to laugh because it's hilarious to hear him speak like an adult, but my body is too stressed.

"How about something else? I could buy you a new book or a puzzle."

"I'll think about it." This time I manage to smile through my heartache.

When we arrive at Mrs. Foster's house, she's already waiting for Clark on the porch. I hand my son over and she gives him a hug. Clark has finally cheered up and now looks forward to spending the day with his adopted grandmother.

"Zoe," Mrs. Foster calls when I walk back to the car.

"Yes?" I brace myself for whatever is coming. Every time someone calls my name, I always expect something negative.

"I like the new hair." She smiles. "It suits you."

"I don't like it," Clark cuts in. "I like the other hair she had yesterday."

I let the comment slide, thank her, and watch as she and Clark walk into the house hand in hand. One thing that makes it all better is knowing that we have Mrs. Foster and she's always there for us. I appreciate the fact that I do not have to worry about getting a babysitter, who might start snooping around in our business.

On the way to Lemon, my mind is racing so much that I almost run a red light. I catch myself in time but still kick myself inwardly. I cannot make stupid mistakes like that.

Before I enter Lemon, I force myself to look as though I'm not feeling well, so Tasha doesn't think I lied. I don't have to try hard. In the rearview mirror, I see that my eyes are empty and have dark bags underneath them. The washed-out look I got from the new hair also helps my case.

Inside the restaurant, my body vibrates with anxiety. I feel as though everyone is watching me, seeing through me, figuring me out.

"Thank you so much for coming in." Tasha is about to give me a hug, but she steps back. I have a feeling she thinks we are friends. She never treats me like an employee. "We need you until 1:00. Is that okay?"

"Sure." I glance at the clock. It's 10:00 a.m. This will be the longest three hours of my life.

I get to work immediately, but this time I'm not giving my all. I want to, and I try my best, but I don't have the strength.

The little voice inside my head refuses to shut up, warning me that I'm about to be exposed. At one point, that voice is so loud I come to a standstill in the middle of the restaurant, a full tray balanced on my hand.

"Are you all right?" one of the waitresses asks me as she walks by. I immediately snap out of it.

In a trance, I take orders and serve meals, all

the while trying to avoid making eye contact with anyone.

"That's not what I ordered," a boy of about seven years old with thick hair sticking out from around his head looks up at me with a look of disgust. "I wanted potato wedges, not stupid French fries."

I swallow hard and glance down at my notepad, which is resting on my tray. He's right. I brought him the wrong order.

The woman, who is probably his mother, pushes the plate in my direction.

Tasha walks by, glancing at us.

I can't afford to make mistakes. I can't put my job on the line.

"I'm so sorry." I pick up the plate of French fries.

At least I got the woman's order right, roasted hake with a green salad. I place the food in front of her.

"What do you expect me to do?" she asks. "Do you want me to start eating without my son? By the time his food gets here, which could be forever, I'll be done eating. And if I wait, my food will go cold."

I inhale a frustrated breath, filling my lungs with fragrant coffee. "I'll make sure it's done quickly. I'm sorry again."

I return to the kitchen.

"Hang in there, Zoe." Tasha appears from behind me. "A few more hours and you'll be done." Her voice is understanding, but I feel terrible.

"I'm sorry." I drag a palm down one side of my face. "I'm just not feeling too well... migraine."

"Raphael keeps some Excedrin in the back. He probably wouldn't mind if you took some," she says. The look of concern she gives me makes me hate myself.

"I did. It didn't help."

"I'm sorry that I had to drag you out here. But as you can see, the place is bursting at the seams."

She's right. The restaurant is loud with silverware clinking against plates on the tables, the gurgle of water glasses being filled, and the voices mixing with the sound of the music from the radio.

I give her an apologetic smile. "Don't worry. I'm fine."

Tasha squeezes my shoulder and gets back to work.

When I serve the boy his golden-brown potato wedges, he doesn't bother to thank me.

When they finally finish their meals and are ready to leave, the woman bluntly informs me that I'll not be getting a tip.

"The food was okay, but the service needs improvement."

Tasha overhears the conversation and comes over to apologize to the woman on my behalf. She flat-out refuses to accept the apology and grabs her son's hand. We watch them storm out of the restaurant.

"I don't know why she's making such a big fuss." Tasha's voice is on edge. "It's not as if we tried to poison her son."

Every time I hear the word *poison*, my throat starts to close up.

"I'm sorry I messed up," I say.

I broke my own rule. Do not mess up at work. Today I failed myself and her.

"Stop that." Tasha gives my arm a gentle slap. "Mistakes happen, and that wasn't even a big one."

For the rest of my shift, I make sure to do everything right. I deliver the right meals and hand back the right change. I don't make anyone angry.

An hour before my shift ends, one of the customers gestures for me to come to the table. He's an older man with a tweed jacket and hair swept from one side of his head to the other to cover up a bald patch.

"Sweetheart, would you mind turning up the volume?" He points at the TV bolted to the wall.

I nod with a smile and turn to go on the search for the remote control.

But the moment I raise my gaze to the TV, I freeze. My face is in a corner of the screen. Instead of doing what the man requested, I head to the tiny staff room and yank off my apron. My hands are trembling and I'm so dizzy, I need to get out in the fresh air before I faint.

When I'm about to leave the staff room, I almost collide with Tasha.

"I'm so sorry," I croak. "I need... I need to go now. I'm really sorry, Tasha."

Before she can respond, I head for the door.

CHAPTER 12

❧

As I'm rummaging inside my bag for my car keys, I bump into someone. Without lifting my head to see who it is, I mumble an apology and push past.

"That's all right." The familiar male voice makes me turn, but only for a brief second before avoiding eye contact again.

It's Officer Tim Roland. He's wearing a uniform this time and looks even more handsome than the first time I saw him.

"You all right?" he calls out.

"Yes, thanks," I respond and speed up, sweat trickling down my spine. It's a good thing I'm leaving now. The last person I need to make any kind of contact with is a police officer. If I didn't leave when I did, I would probably have done so when he walked into the restaurant.

When I get into the car, I release the breath I didn't know I was holding and sink into the warm leather seat.

I drive carefully even though I'm dying to push the car to its limit.

I'm approaching a red traffic light opposite the White Cross Baptist Church when I glance in the rearview mirror and my chest stutters.

A police car is trailing me. My instinct tells me it's Officer Roland.

What if he's investigating me? What if that's the reason why he struck up a conversation with me the other day? What if by colliding with him, I raised some flags?

After the light turns green, he flashes his lights and I pull over.

He's a cop, and I have to obey.

Feeling sick to my stomach, I listen to the thud of his boots on the pavement, counting each step until he reaches my car.

Maybe it's nothing. I could have a broken taillight I didn't notice.

Stop kidding yourself, the little voice scoffs.

I take several deep breaths, forcing myself to stay calm.

When he reaches my car, he plants a gloved hand on the roof. It is, indeed, Officer Roland.

Sweat is pouring from every pore of my body.

"Looks like you need this." He reaches into his pocket and hands me a bone-white handkerchief.

"Thanks." The word comes out in a whisper.

I keep my eyes averted as I dab at my face, careful not to remove the heavy makeup I wear to disguise myself.

"Are you sure you're all right?" he asks again.

"Did I do something wrong, Officer?" I ask and instantly wonder if that was the wrong thing to say. "I mean...yes, I'm fine." My lips tremble into a fake smile.

"Good to hear." He folds his arms over his chest. "Now, why would you think you've done something wrong?"

When I don't respond because I can't find the right words, he clears his throat and continues. "You did nothing wrong, Zoe, right? You looked unwell at the restaurant. I thought you might need some help."

"Yeah, I'm Zoe. Umm...you don't need to be concerned. I'm fine."

He lowers himself to the level of my car window and scrutinizes me with his piercing eyes. "Why don't I believe you?" He straightens up again. "You still don't look well."

That's because I'm nearing the verge of fainting, I want to say, but I keep the words inside my head.

"You're right. I'm not feeling too well today. I have a terrible migraine."

"Then it might not be a good idea for you to drive. Migraines can be a pain." He chuckles.

"I'm good enough to drive," I say quickly.

"How far do you live?"

Wrong question. I don't want him to know where I live. I'm sure he's already heard about the widow from the cabin, but he probably doesn't know yet that it's me.

"Not far." I let out a nervous giggle. "I'll be home soon."

"Good, I'll drive behind you. I want to make sure you arrive safely."

"Please don't trouble yourself. I'm sure you have more important work to do."

"I'm on a break. I was actually looking forward to a cup of coffee at Lemon, but I prefer to help folks out when I can."

I clutch my hands in my lap, unsure what more to tell him. I'm not allowed to say the things I really want to say because he's a police officer and I'm a wanted woman.

"That's very kind. Thank you." I have no choice but to accept the offer, but I'm freaking out. I'm almost hyperventilating as I watch him walking back to his car.

This is bad, a train wreck waiting to happen,

but I can't stop it.

He drives behind me as he promised he would.

My plan was to go to Mrs. Foster's to pick up Clark, but it might not be a good idea anymore. I don't want Officer Roland to know that I have a son.

Afraid to arrive at my cabin, I drive slowly. But eventually, the distance closes between me and my borrowed home. Before long, we're both turning into a dirt road that leads to the cabin.

I'm aware of everything, the tall trees on either side of my car, the dusty sand beneath my car's wheels, the hot air that makes my clothes stick to my skin.

I pull up in front of the cabin and get out of my car. The police officer does the same.

Instead of coming up to me, he slams the door of his car and stands next to it. A finger is on his lips as he gazes at the cabin. "This is where you live?" he asks in a tone that gives nothing away.

"Yep. That's my home."

"A pretty damaged home." He looks it up and down. Outside, the paint is peeling, and a portion of the wall is water stained. Some of the other defects are not immediately noticeable to him. It's a pretty cabin, but it needs a lot of work.

"Looks can be deceiving. The inside isn't so bad." Only if I invite him in will he get to see the chipped bathroom tiles, the discolored walls, or the missing baseboards. I've done a lot in the past months to make it more comfortable for us, but what really matters is that it's private and the price is right. For that we're grateful.

In another life, I'd probably invite him in, so I can make him the coffee he missed at his lunch break, but that would be asking for trouble.

My phone is ringing inside my bag. It has to be Tasha wanting to know what's going on with me.

Guilt stabs me when I think of what I did to her, leaving her hanging when she needed me most.

What would she do if she found out that I'd been lying to her for months about who I really am? She would probably fire me if she hasn't already.

Officer Roland attempts to make small talk, but he soon figures out that I'm not in the mood to chat, so he gives me a small nod and gets back into his car.

Before he drives off, I do come to my senses and thank him for his help.

"No problem." He sticks his head out the window. "It's my job to serve and protect."

I smile and turn to the cabin, but he calls after me. When I turn back to him, he grins. "Your new hairstyle is nice."

My hand goes to my head. I totally forgot that the last time he saw me I had a different look. And yet he recognized me immediately. That cannot be a good sign.

I breathe life back into my numb body and force myself to act normal. After all, people change their looks all the time.

"Thanks." I give him a wave as he drives away.

I pray that he will not return to check up on me.

Safely inside, I return Tasha's call and apologize.

"Zoe, that wasn't okay."

"I'm truly sorry."

"I get that you're not feeling well, but for you to run out like that? You could have just rested in the office."

I press a hand to my forehead. The headache I lied about having is slowly becoming real. "I couldn't stay. I'm sorry."

"Something is not right with you," she says. "Is there anything you want to talk to me about?"

"No." The word comes flooding out. "There's nothing. I'm fine. I'll be fine."

"You can trust me, Zoe. I hope you know that."

She has a good heart, but I can't trust her. I can't trust anyone at this point. I'm desperate to lean on someone, but what I want and what I need to do are in conflict.

I cannot let my mask slip under any circumstances.

After a short silence, she speaks again. "Maybe it's none of my business, but when you said you had a migraine, it didn't seem like you were telling the truth. Seems like you've got something more going on, something emotional."

I have to give her something, something she can hold on to so she doesn't continue digging.

"Being a single mother is tough sometimes," I say. It's as close to the truth as I'm willing to get. I can't tell her that being a single mom and on the run is even harder.

"I know it is." She pauses, then sighs. "You know what, go ahead and take a few days off. We'll manage."

I swallow the tears lingering in my throat. "Thank you."

When we hang up, I run to the kitchen and pour myself a glass of water. My throat is parched.

I should go and pick up Clark, but it's not safe for me to drive again, and I don't want him to see me in this state.

I need to be alone, to think.

Instead of sitting idle, I sit in front of the TV and flip through the channels. Sooner or later, Brett's murder will be reported again. Forty minutes pass before one of the news channels features it.

According to the reporters, the police department in Fort Haven has been getting calls from people who claim to have seen me. They don't elaborate, so I can't tell if the callers are from Willow Creek or another town.

Breathe, just breathe.

There are many people who would lie for a reward of $20,000.

Since I don't have to go to work for a few days, I'll avoid going out.

Desperate to bring my body back from its numb state before Clark comes home, I run myself a bath. I fill the tub with cold water and sink into it, submerging my head and face.

What if I just eliminated myself from this world before the cops or Cole find me?

But how could I do that to Clark?

It's not the first time I've thought of suicide. It was a constant thought growing up in the foster care system, but also throughout my marriage when Cole made my life a nightmare.

When my lungs start to scream for oxygen, I emerge from the water, splashing it everywhere, gasping for air.

As soon as my breathing finally gets back to normal, the doorbell rings, and goose pimples erupt on my skin. Cold fear sweeps through me.

I almost slip as I climb out of the tub and shrug on a bathrobe.

After debating on what to do for a few painful heartbeats, I open the door, thinking it might be Officer Roland again. He knows I'm home.

It's not him. It's no one.

All I find is a single, pristine white feather lying on the wooden porch. It doesn't have to mean anything. I live in the woods, after all. But what about the doorbell ringing? Was that real, or am I hearing things? To avoid going crazy, I convince myself that the sound was all in my head.

CHAPTER 13

Burying my head in the sand won't get me anywhere. It's time to take action.

Cole is the key. My gut tells me he not only killed Janella, but also his own son. I need to prove his guilt before the police catch up with me. I need to gather evidence that would prove my innocence.

Instead of running from my past, it's time I face it head-on.

I grab one of the notepads lying around the cabin and a pen. Then I sink onto the couch and write down everything that pops into my head about the night that my life changed forever.

Brett had clearly told me that the medication he wanted me to inject into his veins would not be detectable during an autopsy. I still don't get why it was. Unless he lied to me. It doesn't make sense.

I suddenly remember that I heard sounds

that night and thought it was the branches outside the house.

What if it wasn't? What if it was someone else in the house aside from me, Brett, and Clark?

What if it was Cole? Maybe he had brought his own deadly cocktail to kill his son with. I write everything down.

Another question that lingers on my mind is why Cole would want to kill his son. They didn't have much of a relationship. He loved Brett for the mere reason that he derived power from controlling him and making him feel small. But I don't think he would have wanted him dead.

When my head is empty, I flip through the channels again, but there are no more reports on the murder.

I need more information to help me put the puzzle together.

I need the internet, but I can't go back to Lemon. There is a library a few blocks from where Mrs. Foster lives with computers that people can use.

I'll stop by before I buy groceries and pick up Clark.

Before I leave the cabin, I dress in black jeans, a black T-shirt, a cap, and sunglasses.

It's a relief to find that there's only one other

person at the library. I still go for a computer at the back of the room.

At first, I read the articles, noting any information I deem important. Then I start watching videos of news snippets.

I stumble upon a video of a Fort Haven reporter interviewing Marjorie Smith, our neighbor who was standing in her garden the morning I drove away with Clark. In the video, she claims to have been with Cole when they found Janella's body. It's the first time I'm hearing of it, and I find it suspicious.

I remove my glasses and pinch the bridge of my nose. This new information makes everything much more complicated. The more people that are involved in this web, the harder it will be to uncover the truth.

Either way, I jot everything down, wondering why Marjorie didn't come forward earlier.

The only explanation is that the cops are becoming suspicious of Cole's version of events and he found an alibi to support his story. It made sense that he'd choose Marjorie. The woman had always had a crush on him. Every time Cole showed up at our house, Marjorie found a reason to drop by with some sweet treat for him. When Cole didn't visit for a while, she would ask Brett when he would come again. She hardly ever spoke to me.

"Finding a dead body is the hardest thing I have ever experienced. I still haven't recovered from the trauma." She pats her perfect updo. Her bright smile contradicts the words coming from her mouth.

Something is different about her, but I can't figure out what it is.

"Cole is a kind and wonderful man. I was glad to be by his side during that difficult time."

"In your opinion, do you think it's possible that Mr. Wilton's wife killed her own husband and the–"

"There's no doubt in my mind. She married Brett for his money. Everyone knows that. She used to work as a maid at Mr. Wilton's hotel. Did you know?"

Anger pounding through me, I close the video. The torture is too much for me to handle.

Marjorie had once made a casual comment that her daughter and Brett had been friends for years and she always thought they would end up becoming more. It's clear she wanted Cole for herself and Brett for her daughter, and I had just stepped in and destroyed that dream for her.

But right now, she might be the only person who can give me the answers I need.

Without wasting time, I type in the Fort Haven town website address.

The site boasts the local attractions, yearly events, and even a phone directory that enables locals to stay in touch in order to strengthen the bond of the community.

I click on the phone directory page and scroll to the letter S.

I don't know yet what I want to ask Marjorie, but I feel as though she's an important key in this whole mess.

When I recall her petting her perfectly coiffed hair during the interview, an idea hits me.

Instead of calling her on my phone, I drive to the nearest payphone. I'd gotten rid of my old cell when we went on the run and picked up a prepaid phone. It's hard for burners to be traced, but it's not impossible. I don't want to take chances.

Ignoring the stench of urine in the little cubicle, I slide a coin into the machine. I don't recall the last time I used a payphone and it feels strange.

As soon as the phone starts ringing, it's picked up. "Marjorie Smith at your service. How can I help?" She has clearly rehearsed on the off chance that the press will contact her.

"Hello," I say, holding my nose to disguise

the real sound of my voice. "My name is Linda Simone from the Fort Haven Tribune. I was informed that you are willing to answer questions pertaining to the murder of Mr. Brett Wilton and his housekeeper."

"That's right," Marjorie chirps. "I will do anything that assists in the capture of the murderer."

I'm silent for a moment, the back of my throat aching with rage. "Ma'am, I will not waste your time, so let's jump right in."

"Perfect," she says. "Would you mind it very much if at the end of the interview you give me an email address? I'd like to send you the photo I want you to use. I got some new headshots."

I have never met anyone who loves themselves so much, aside from Cole, of course.

"Sure, no problem." It's a struggle to keep calm. But this is my chance. I can't blow it. "Will you please explain to me exactly what happened that day."

She clears her throat. "Well, as I told the police and other reporters, I was in my garden, tending to my plants, when I saw Mrs. Wilton driving off in a hurry. At the same time, I saw Mr. Wilton, the deceased's father, arriving at the house. I remember thinking it was strange that his daughter-in-law would leave when he was coming over. I'm positive that she saw his car."

"What do you believe the reason was?" I ask.

"The woman is guilty of murder and she felt uncomfortable coming face-to-face with her father-in-law. Only a guilty person would run."

"And do you believe that Meghan Wilton also killed the housekeeper?"

"Who else could have murdered that poor girl? Cole certainly didn't do it." It's the first time I'm hearing her refer to him by his first name. She had always called him Mr. Wilton. They must have grown closer over the past year.

"You mentioned that you and Mr. Cole Wilton found the housekeeper's body. Am I correct?"

"Yes. Cole was sitting in his car for quite some time, so I decided to go and see if he was all right. We are close friends, you know."

I almost laugh out loud. Cole couldn't care less about her. She was too infatuated to see it.

"No, I had no idea." I mutter. "Did you suggest accompanying him into the house?"

"I did. I understand why he found it hard to enter the house alone. It was the place where his son died. He was brokenhearted."

I release my nose and draw in a deep breath.

No more beating around the bush. "Miss Smith, there are speculations that you received compensation in exchange for being Mr. Wilton's alibi. Do you care to comment on that?"

Silence.

"Miss Smith, are you still there?"

"What exactly are you accusing me of?" The charming voice is long gone.

"Lying." My tone is firm. "Were you paid to lie?"

"How dare you!"

The phone goes dead.

It's fine. She answered my question without saying a word.

CHAPTER 14

Taking matters into my own hands gives me a burst of energy I haven't felt in a while.

When I arrive at Mrs. Foster's house to pick up Clark, the anxiety that had loomed over me earlier has dimmed. I'm still terrified of the police catching up with me, but I won't go down without a fight. And I'll make damn sure that Cole is not painted to be the innocent man they all think he is. He deserves to be behind bars.

The loss of his freedom could lead to me getting my own back.

Mrs. Foster is not out on the porch with Clark like she normally is.

I get out of the car and walk up to the door, ringing the bell twice. It takes a while for her to come to the door. When she does, she's all smiles.

"Sorry, darling, I didn't hear the bell. We were out in the back, planting marigolds."

"I have my own flower bed, Mommy." Clark emerges from behind Mrs. Foster.

"Is that so?" I throw her a quick smile. "That sounds like fun."

"So much fun! Mrs. Foster said she's going to get more seeds for us tomorrow."

"But we're celebrating your birthday tomorrow, Superboy. We'll be spending the day together, remember?" Clark's birthday was actually three months ago, but I was going through a severe bout of depression at the time and was unable to give him the attention he deserved. It was his idea to pretend it's his birthday tomorrow.

Clark's face crumples, but only for a second before he perks up again. It would have crushed me if he would rather spend time with Mrs. Foster than with me. I wouldn't have blamed him, though. She's the person he spends the majority of his time with.

"Why don't you do something different today?" Mrs. Foster rests a hand on top of Clark's head.

"What do you mean?" I tilt my head to the side.

"Instead of rushing back to the cabin, I was thinking maybe the two of you could have an early dinner with me. It's been a while."

"I'm not sure." I shift from one foot to the

other. Although I appreciate her invitation, I was looking forward to being alone with Clark. "We kind of have plans."

"Plans can be changed. I would certainly appreciate the company." Her eyes are pleading.

Mrs. Foster is such a lovely person and my heart really goes out to her. She lost her husband only three years ago, and she has no children to keep her company. That's why she loves it so much when Clark comes to visit.

I think of insisting that we have to go, but the weary look in the woman's eyes makes me change my mind. How could I refuse her an hour or two of my time?

"You're right. Plans can be changed." I step into the house that always smells of fresh laundry. "Have you already cooked something?"

"Not yet." She laughs. "Silly me. The idea to invite you to dinner just came to me now. I haven't even given thought to what I will feed you. I'll come up with something."

It's already close to 6:00 p.m. and when Mrs. Foster cooks, she takes forever. We've been to her place for dinner four times before and we ended up staying for over three hours.

As I'm closing the door behind me, an idea comes to me. "How about I cook us something? You relax."

Since I know my way around her kitchen already, it won't be hard to find a few random ingredients and rustle up a quick meal.

She lays a hand on her chest. "I can't let you do that. *You* need to rest. You've been working all day. It must have been busy at the restaurant for Tasha to let you work longer than you'd planned."

Guilt gnaws at my insides like acid. She doesn't know that I left work early.

"That's all right." I wave a dismissive hand. "I have enough energy left."

"Can you cook lasagna?" Clark asks and my cheeks burn with embarrassment.

"It depends on what Mrs. Foster has in the kitchen." I glance at her again, questioningly. "And if I'm allowed to cook."

Mrs. Foster gives my arm a pat. "If it's really no bother, I would appreciate that."

While Clark and Mrs. Foster are back in the garden tending to their flower beds, I rummage around in the kitchen in search of ingredients. I don't find anything for lasagna, so I decide to cook fried rice with vegetables and chicken instead.

While I cook, I try to clear my mind of everything that happened earlier. I also make myself a promise that when I'm with my son,

I'll do my best to be present. It's going to be hard, but I'll give it my all.

When they return to the kitchen in time for the food, they're both smiling from ear to ear.

"It all smells wonderful. Why did I ever try to keep you from cooking dinner?" Mrs. Foster throws back her head in laughter. "One day, when you open up that restaurant or bakery, I'll be one of your first customers."

I give her a smile and distract myself with serving the food. Thinking about the future doesn't come easy to me, not when there's such a huge obstacle between me and everything I want. It's safer to only focus on surviving the present.

"Clark, is this better than lasagna?" I ask.

He nods and shoves a spoonful of food into his mouth, his eyes dancing.

Mrs. Foster and I smile at each other. Right now, in Mrs. Foster's cozy kitchen, I feel normal. I feel free even though at any moment, my joy could be stolen from my heart and replaced with pain and fear.

But the few minutes that I have to enjoy the moment, I pretend we're a family, me, Clark, and Mrs. Foster. In my mind, I pretend she's the mother I never had and Clark's grandmother. The way she talks to him and the way she touches him makes it easy for me to fool myself.

I'm about to serve the dessert I whipped up when the doorbell rings.

Mrs. Foster frowns. "That's odd. I'm not expecting visitors. Who would visit at this hour?" She wipes her mouth and pushes back her chair. "I'll be right back, dears."

I glance at the kitchen clock. It's close to eight. The time has gone by so fast.

I secretly pray that Mrs. Foster won't invite the person in. I want to remain in our safe bubble a little longer.

While Clark continues to eat, I strain my ears to listen to Mrs. Foster speaking to the person at the door. The male voice sounds angry.

I'm unable to catch the words because the man is barking them out at a high speed and Mrs. Foster is lowering her voice.

I jolt at the sound of the door slamming. Everything is silent until suddenly, someone throws something at the kitchen window.

Clark drops his spoon and we both turn to look. Our eyes meet those of an angry man with long, greasy hair and tattoos on one side of his neck.

"Mommy, I'm scared." Clark runs over to me and hides his face in my chest.

"It's all right, baby," I say.

The man sneers at me, then flips me off

before stumbling away as if he's drunk.

Who is he, and what did he want from Mrs. Foster? What did she do to anger him so much that he had to extend his anger to me?

Before I can come up with answers, Mrs. Foster returns to the kitchen. She's not the same woman who had left and the sparkle in her eyes has disappeared.

I want to tell her what the man did at the window, but she's upset enough.

"Who was it?" I ask, desperate to know.

"Nobody." She wipes her hands on a kitchen towel as if she had washed them. "No one at all."

When she turns around again, her eyes are wet. "I hope you don't mind, but I'm rather tired already." She forces a laugh. "Old age is certainly catching up with me. Please feel free to stay and enjoy your dessert. I apologize for being such a terrible host."

With that, she kisses Clark on the top of the head and squeezes my shoulder. Then she shuffles out of the kitchen. With her shoulders hunched, she looks much shorter.

It feels uncomfortable to be eating dessert without her around, so I tell Clark we should go. He doesn't want to leave, but I don't give him a choice. I do my best to explain to him that Mrs. Foster is not feeling well and she needs to rest. In the end, he groans and folds his arms across his chest. He definitely likes Mrs. Foster more than me, but I can't find it in me to be jealous of the older woman.

Back at the cabin, when I close my eyes to sleep, I see the man from the window again. I feel the fury in his gaze and wonder whether he's a danger to me and my son.

Anyone has the power to cause trouble for us at this point.

CHAPTER 15

❧

I wake up shortly before midnight, unable to sleep.

Frustrated, I slide out of bed, careful not to wake Clark, and sit on the edge of the bed. His gentle breathing is interrupted by an occasional snore.

I want to get back into bed, put my arms around him, and make him a silent promise that everything will be all right. But I'm cautious about making promises I might not be able to keep. I take it one day at the time, only making promises that don't expire beyond a day. It's safer that way and it protects Clark from further disappointments.

I rise to my feet and it suddenly occurs to me that something actually woke me up. It wasn't a nightmare. I tiptoe out of the room and close the door behind me, heading to the kitchen.

It's late, but the only thing that would calm

me down is baking. I planned on waking up early anyway to bake Clark's cake. Since I'm already awake, I might as well do it now. I gather all the ingredients I need and jump right in.

A snapping sound catches my attention. It's coming from outside. The blinds are closed and I'm afraid to peek.

Standing still at the stove, my ears strain to listen to more sounds, and every muscle in my body is on high alert.

I'm dreaming. I'm making it all up. It's not the first time I imagine something that's not there. The missing cupcake comes to mind.

I did it as a kid. Whenever I was particularly stressed, hallucinations followed.

"Get out of your head, child," Mrs. Harris, one of my many foster parents, used to snap when I told her I was afraid of the monsters in my head. "That head of yours will get you in trouble one day," she'd say.

When I don't hear anything else, I exhale and get back to my baking, burying my hands into the silky flour.

Within minutes, the mixture is ready, and the aromas of vanilla, chocolate, and mint make me smile.

Maybe I should have waited to bake the cake with Clark, to create another memory together, but he also loves surprises. He'll love the cake.

But that's not enough. I'm taking him out, too. Going out fills me with dread, but it's his birthday. He begged me to take him to the park, and I felt terrible to hear my son beg to be outdoors. Toys no longer interest him as much as the freedom to be a child.

A memory from the past comes to me.

On Clark's third birthday, Brett and I took him to Disneyland. To my horror, we discovered that Cole was also there, staying at the same hotel, for the same period of time.

I had asked Brett not to share our plans with his dad. It was a chance to be just the three of us, and I wanted to enjoy my family without Cole's constant shadow.

Somehow, he knew. Janella had told him, he said, and he wanted to surprise us. He didn't get the reaction he expected from me. The whole weekend was ruined. Cole ended up stealing the show, buying gifts for Clark that cost a fortune, like a toy train that Clark loved so much he took it almost everywhere with him. It's the only toy he brought with him from Fort Haven.

I'll do whatever I can to make this birthday special. I'll give him another missing piece of his childhood, a happy memory to keep him going.

The silence around me is so thick. It confirms that the sounds I heard earlier were not real.

While the cake is baking, I sit at the kitchen table with the notes I made about Cole.

My eyes scan the page, where I scribbled down my conversation with Marjorie. I did call her back after she hung up on me, but she didn't pick up. I took that as a sign that I was right, and she had lied for Cole.

I'm not done digging.

Another call I want to make is straight to the source. He loved his hotels even more than he had loved his own son. The answers could be where his heart is.

I circle the phone number of the housekeeping department of the Fort Haven Black Oyster Hotel.

Since I'll be taking Clark out of town to a park we've never been to before, I'll find a payphone and make the call.

I don't plan to speak to Cole, but I have someone else in mind who might be able to give me the answers I need. I'll destroy him before he gets a chance to get to me.

I'm far more terrified of him than I am of the cops.

Another sound makes me gasp. I straighten up so fast my back cracks. Before I can figure out what the sound is, the blinds start to glow as though someone is pointing a bright light at the window, car headlights perhaps.

Someone is out there. It's Cole. He has found me.

As I push to my feet, fear chills me to the bone.

I run to the switch, flick off the light, and press my back against the wall. The room remains illuminated by the light outside seconds before the lights go out again. Just as my eyes are adjusting to the darkness, whoever is outside turns the light back on.

My mouth grows drier with each second.

He's out there playing some kind of game. The lights continue to go on and off until they finally stay on for longer than a minute.

My heart is lodged inside my throat now. I want to scream, but I don't want to wake Clark. Luckily the bedroom is on the other side of the cabin, or he would wake up from the bright light.

Cole is dangerous. Maybe I should call 911. But what if the cops arrive and I end up being the one going away in handcuffs?

I can't let them take me away. I can't leave Clark.

I run to the block of knives and remove the largest one. The light on the other side of the window is still shining bright.

What is he waiting for? Is he enjoying taunting me before he shows me his face?

Panic brings my body to life, and I run through the entire cabin, checking that all the windows are closed. Then I look in the bedroom to make sure Clark is okay. He's still fast asleep. But for how long?

I return to the kitchen and force myself to move to the window. He's taunting me again, switching the light on and off again. Then they stay on.

A car door slams and my stomach clenches. He's coming to get me. I'm already imagining him kicking down the back door.

I need to protect my son from him. My hand tightens around the handle of the knife, and I hold my breath as I open the blinds a few inches.

He's standing in front of a pickup truck, surrounded by light. The light is blinding me, making it hard for me to see his face. But I feel his eyes on me. In one hand I have the knife, and in the other, my cell phone in case I'm forced to call 911.

He starts walking toward the kitchen window. My mind tells me to let go of the blinds, but I can't get myself to. My hand feels paralyzed. When he emerges from the harshness of the light and comes close enough to the kitchen window, I catch my breath.

It's not Cole.

It's the man with the tattoos, the man who had looked at me through the kitchen window of Mrs. Foster's kitchen. He's looking at me the same way now.

This time, he gives me that creepy sneer, then turns to walk back to his truck. He slides behind the wheel and starts the engine. Then he drives off.

The knife slips from my hand and I jump back before the tip slices my bare foot. Weak with fear, I crumple to the floor, my hands covering my mouth.

Who is he? And what does he want from me? It's exhausting to think I will have to worry about someone else now on top of Cole. I don't think I have the energy.

Mrs. Foster is probably the only person who can tell me who the stranger is, but the way she looked after he showed up at her house, it's probably not something she wants to talk about.

But he scares the hell out of me. Without saying a word, he threatened our safety.

I make sure the doors and windows are locked again, feeling crazy because I know they are. Then I open the kitchen blinds and gaze down the path where his truck disappeared.

My eyes are still blurry from being assaulted by the bright lights, and my heart feels like it's cowering in a corner of my body, afraid to come out. Not even baking can help how I'm feeling right now. I switch off the oven. The cake will be ruined, but I can't finish. The magic is gone.

The only thing I want to do is lie next to my son.

I slide into bed and tighten an arm around his warm, little body. I'm holding him, but he's the one that's holding me together.

CHAPTER 16

Almost a week after the stranger showed up at the cabin, I'm back to work. He never came back, but he left me on edge and unable to sleep much at night, always waiting for the sound of tires on the path outside.

What hurt the most was the fact that I was so tormented to the point that Clark's birthday didn't go as planned.

I managed to finish the football chocolate cake. I sang to him and we danced around, but I wasn't there at all mentally, and he felt it. Everything was ruined again. I couldn't fake being happy and excited, and I found it hard to focus on him when my emotions were in turmoil.

Clark asked me several times if I was all right. It killed me inside. I had failed him yet again.

I've been waiting every day for the man to return, but he never did.

Until now.

He's standing in the doorway of Lemon. The same greasy hair brushes his shoulders, the same sneer stretches across his lips as our eyes meet.

I'm tempted to run, but I can't do it again. I can't let Tasha down.

Exhaustion is pressing down my shoulders. In addition to being constantly terrified that Cole might find us, I also have to be afraid of someone I don't even know.

"Great," Tasha says next to me. "Just what we need today."

Her eyes are on my tormentor, who is now making his way toward one of the tables in the back. Once seated, he reaches into his back pocket for a pack of cigarettes. He pulls one from the pack and lights it.

"Hell no." Tasha charges toward the table. I can't hear what she's telling him, but her expression says it all.

To my horror, while still keeping his eyes on her face, he turns the cigarette upside down and presses the glowing tip into the table. Smoke curls upward as it burns through the tablecloth.

"Get out of here now." Tasha nearly shouts as she yanks the tablecloth off the table.

The man stands and looks past her in my

direction. When he finally walks out, I start to panic. What if he waits for me outside?

He's definitely out to get me. Why else would he come to my workplace?

I thought of bringing him up in conversation with Mrs. Foster when I dropped off Clark, but she was on the phone and I was late for work. My plan was to ask her about him this evening.

"If he weren't Mrs. Foster's son, I swear I would have called the cops on him." Tasha's chest is rising and falling as she makes her way back to me. "It's hard to believe that someone like that could come from such a gentle and kind woman." She hugs the folded tablecloth to her body.

"Mrs. Foster has a son?" The revelation sends a ripple of surprise through me. I don't understand. She clearly told me that she doesn't have kids.

Tasha hands the cover to one of the other waitresses. "Yes, his name is Ronan. I'm surprised you didn't know that." She frowns at me. "I assumed you did since you and Mrs. Foster are pretty close."

"I *did* see him…once. But I don't know him."

"Well, it's in your best interest to keep as far away from him as you can." At the sound of someone coming through the door, she turns away from me. "Let's talk in a bit. My favorite guests have arrived. I'll serve them personally."

It's Martha and Julius, a couple in their nineties who come to Lemon every single Monday at the same time. They also order the same meal every time, potato and tuna casserole, which they eat while holding hands.

It's very sweet. But I can't find joy in anything today.

Tasha leaves me standing by the bar, trying to process what I heard.

I finally pull myself together and serve a group of teenagers.

"One grilled cheese sandwich, one hamburger with fries." I write everything down so I don't make a mistake again. My head is a mess.

I find Tasha in the kitchen, passing on her order to Raphael. "I didn't know Mrs. Foster had kids," I say.

"Well, you saw him. I wouldn't be surprised if she wants to pretend he doesn't exist. Word around town is that he killed his twin brother."

"Oh my God. That's... That's scary." My mind goes back to the night he parked in front of the cabin, sending me a warning I didn't understand. "Why isn't he in prison?"

"He was never found guilty. The story is that

a few years ago, he went boating with his brother, Daniel, and only he returned. But apparently, the police had never been able to find enough evidence to nail him. He *did* just come out of prison for something else, though. Assault, I think." Tasha pours iced tea into several glasses and places them on the silver tray. She balances it on her flat palm. "I feel sorry for Mrs. Foster. He really made her life hell. People are hoping he'll commit another crime just so he'll go back to prison and leave her alone."

Tasha walks away, leaving me staring after her, shaken by what she's told me. I get it now. His mother wants nothing to do with him, and he's taking it out on me. On one hand, I'm relieved that he has nothing to do with my past, but on the other, he might end up blowing my cover. If he continues to stalk me, he might discover things I don't want him to know.

The rest of the day passes in a blur, and when I go to pick up Clark, I find Ronan's truck parked in front of the house across from Mrs. Foster's.

He's sitting inside, smoke from a cigarette curling in wisps out the window. His gaze is focused on the house. He may not be welcome in his mother's home, but that won't stop him from spying on her.

What if he does something to her? If he's capable of killing his own brother, she might be in danger. But then again, what can I do to protect her from him? The only person I have the power to protect is Clark.

I'm glad Tasha told me because now I can remain alert. If he shows up at the cabin again, I might call the cops. For the first time, I wish that I had made friends with Officer Roland.

I try not to look at Ronan's truck as I make my way down the path to Mrs. Foster's door. But his gaze is burning holes in my back, like two cigarette burns.

While I wait for Mrs. Foster to open the door, I glance over my shoulder briefly and he gives me a curt nod.

I turn away, my hands sweating as I ring the bell again. When Mrs. Foster opens the door, I almost faint with relief.

I thank her and she quickly closes the door without acknowledging Ronan. She obviously never wants to let him into her life again. But how will he retaliate?

When I get into my car, I glimpse her peering through the living room window.

You have your own problems. The voice inside my head is urging me to drive away, to leave her behind. There's nothing I can do to protect her from her own son. Especially since I cannot even protect myself.

I drive fast, but I don't head in the direction of the cabin. Clark notices.

"Where are we going, Mommy?" he asks when I don't turn down the dirt road that leads into the woods.

"I thought maybe we could drive around for a bit before it gets dark."

He doesn't object. He appreciates anything that keeps him out of the house. I allow him to choose the music on the radio, and I pretend to be having as much fun as he is.

When I glance in the rearview mirror, I catch sight of a rusty truck. It's Ronan trailing us, trying to scare me again.

Panicked, I drive through unknown streets, trying my best to outrun him without speeding. He follows right behind.

Left with no other choice, I start driving in the direction of the police station. Only then does he disappear. He doesn't show up again for the rest of the day, not even at the cabin, but I know he will.

I can't help thinking that I'm headed for my downfall and Ronan is going to have a large part to play. If he's become this fixated on me, he might be the one who will connect the dots between me and my past and expose me.

CHAPTER 17

Clark and I are hiding out in our cabin. I haven't taken him to Mrs. Foster for two days now, which also means I didn't get to go to work. If staying close to Mrs. Foster means Clark and I might be in danger, I have to keep my distance, even for a while.

"I don't understand," she said over the phone when I told her I wasn't dropping Clark off at her house. "I don't mind taking care of your little boy. Surely you know that."

"Yes," I said. "I do, and I appreciate it so much but–"

"Then what's the problem?"

I squeezed my eyes shut. "Nothing. I just want to spend more time with Clark. I've been working so much."

I wanted to tell Mrs. Foster the truth, but Ronan is her son. It doesn't matter what kind of relationship they have. Nothing will stop him from being her child, and I don't want to come between them.

If I stay away from her, maybe they will rebuild the relationship. I find it hard to believe after everything I heard about Ronan that they will find their way back to each other, but that's not my business. My business is to protect myself and Clark.

I asked for four days off from work. Tasha was disappointed, so I hope that's all it will take for Ronan to lose interest in me. Otherwise I might lose my job.

The only other option is taking Clark with me to work. Tasha wouldn't mind, but it scares me that Ronan might show up and talk to him while I'm busy. I don't want him anywhere near him.

Hopefully, staying away for a bit would give me time to come up with a plan.

"Mommy, do you want to play Memory with me?"

"Yes." I glance up at Clark from a book I'm reading. "But first, I want us to go into town for a bit."

"Can we go to Mrs. Foster today?"

"No, baby. I just need to make a call."

"But you have a phone. There it is." He points at my cell phone on the couch next to me.

"It's not... I don't have enough credit." I

can't tell him that the call I need to make has to be untraceable, and I've been lying to Clark for so long that this one just rolls off my tongue. I hate that it's becoming easier.

"Can we go to the park after you're finished?"

"I'm sorry, sweetie. Can I take a rain check?"

I feel terrible for breaking so many promises to Clark. Since we never got to go out for his birthday redo, I promised that I will make it up to him. Now I'm saying no again.

"But I gave you so many rain checks already." He plants his hands on his hips, his eyes flashing with anger.

But I'm afraid. I'm afraid that the more I put us out there, the more chances we give someone the opportunity to figure out who we are. It's too risky. I hate what I'm doing to my son, but if I go to prison, it would be worse for him.

"You're right." I gesture for him to come closer. "I'm so sorry."

He lays his head on my lap and I stroke his hair, enjoying the warmth of his scalp. He likes it when I soothe him that way.

"This is the last rain check," he murmurs. "Can we go next Saturday? And when I finish playing, can we eat a burger at a restaurant?"

"Okay," I say.

He sits up suddenly, his eyes flashing again, but this time it's with excitement. "You promise?" It doesn't matter how many promises I have broken; he still believes in me. He's still prepared to give me another chance.

"I promise." I kiss his forehead.

I have to keep this one. There's no way I'm going to hurt him again.

Before we get into the car, I scan the surroundings.

Every time I'm in the kitchen at night, I keep expecting to see the blinds glowing from Ronan's headlights. I keep waiting for him to show up at the door, but nothing has happened. Maybe he's leaving me alone. Maybe all he wanted was for me to stay away from his mother.

I buckle Clark into his car seat and slide behind the wheel. In my head, I'm already rehearsing the conversation I'll have with the person who will answer the phone in the Black Oyster housekeeping department.

I should have already called, but I was nervous that the person would recognize my voice and notify Cole. But I haven't given up on trying to find something on him, something damaging enough to land him in prison.

I'm more convinced than ever that he had something to do with Brett's death. The sounds I heard that night could have been him. He had a habit of showing up at random times. There was a day I found him sitting in our living room when I came home from shopping. No one else was home except him. He said he wanted to speak to me. I never gave him the chance. I stayed out of his way until Brett came home and he finally left.

He was in the house that night. I just have to prove it.

*

I don't go to the same payphone I used to call Marjorie. Instead, I drive to a different one. By the time we arrive, Clark is asleep.

He tries to shake me off when I wake him, but I don't want to leave him alone in the car.

Holding the hand of my drowsy son, I approach a phone box with skulls painted on the side. Aside from a dry cleaner and a gas station, there's not much around.

I don't want Clark to hear the conversation, so I give him my phone and earphones so he can play games.

I dial and hold my breath as the phone rings.

"Housekeeping. How may I help you?"

"Hi, my name is Rosemary Fox. I work for the EEOC. I'm calling to ask if you can answer a few questions pertaining to your working environment at the Black Oyster Hotel."

"Sorry, did you say you work for the EEOC?"

"Yes." I pinch the bridge of my nose. "Equal Employment Opportunity Commission."

There's a brief silence. "Oh, and what did you say your name was?"

The woman on the other end is Cindy Barnes. I recognize her voice because it's quite unique—husky and squeaky at the same time.

"My name is Rosemary Fox. I was wondering if you could answer some questions for me. We're conducting research on...on employee harassment." The words coming out of my mouth don't make sense. I'm not even sure if the EEOC contacts companies directly when doing research, but I'm guessing Cindy doesn't know either.

There's another, longer silence.

"Sorry," she says in a clipped voice. "I don't have anything to say."

I can't let her go without getting something out of this phone call, so I search my brain for a question that packs a punch and gets me the answers I need.

"I just have one quick question. Have there been any occurrences in the past that would indicate a hostile working environment at the Black Oyster Hotel in Fort Haven?"

"I don't know what you're talking about," Cindy snaps. Her voice is shaking, which tells me that she's afraid to say the wrong thing.

"Our sources informed us that there's quite a high employee turnover at the hotel, especially among the housekeeping department. Did you have any complaints in advance of their termination or resignation that might indicate a reason?"

I personally know that between the time that Brett was diagnosed with cancer and his death, five housekeeping staff left the hotel. Even while he was sick, Brett was responsible for handling the aftermath of their leaving.

"Ma'am, I'm sorry I'm not able to help you."

"Are you confirming that you are working in a safe environment and there's no cause for concern? Are you sure that you have never observed or experienced harassment from your employer or other employees? I do hope you understand that the only way to end harassment is to speak up."

She hangs up on me. I could choose to see it as a failure, but it isn't. Cindy had said nothing, but at the same time, she said it all.

I have no idea where to go from here, but I need to dig deeper. The best way to do that might be to get in touch with some of the employees who had left the hotel. I need to find out why. I can guess, but I need the truth straight from them, something that cannot be disputed. But who to start with?

Then, one person instantly comes to mind. Denise Sanchez. She used to be my friend until I was asked to stay away from the employees. Soon after, she left the hotel. Prior to her departure, she had worked at the Black Oyster Hotel for five years, one of the longest durations that a housekeeping employee stuck around, as far as I could tell.

I have to find out why she left.

CHAPTER 18

T he doorbell rings. I drop the wooden spoon into the pan, putting the scrambled eggs on hold. I switch off the stove but remain standing in front of it. A trickle of sweat makes its way down my spine.

Anyone could be at the door, Cole, Ronan, or the police. But I didn't hear the sound of a car.

I wish I could see who it is, but the front of the cabin is not visible from the kitchen window.

I lock the back door and shut the kitchen blinds.

Clark watches me from the kitchen table with wide eyes. I place a finger to my lips.

The doorbell rings again and we both stare at the kitchen door.

Fists clenched at my sides, I move to the door, followed by Clark's gaze. In my paranoia, I can already hear the sound of the front door crashing as the police kick it down.

I spin around at the sound of a soft tap-tap at the back door.

My mouth is dry as I tiptoe to it and place my hand on the handle. If only the person on the other side would speak. I need to know who it is.

"Who is it, Mommy?" Clark whispers, and again I hold my shaking finger up to my lips. He looks so scared now, but I can't explain. I can't assure him that everything is all right because I'm not sure.

Is this it? Is this the end of the road? Is my son about to witness me being arrested?

It would be a scar he'd carry for the rest of his life.

The knocking persists, but it's gentle.

I quickly help Clark out of his chair. I'm about to usher him out of the kitchen when I finally hear a voice from the other side of the slab of wood.

"Zoe," the woman calls. "Are you in there?"

My shoulders sink with relief. It's Mrs. Foster. Before I can open the door, Clark runs to it and turns the key.

"We thought it was a bad person." He throws himself into Mrs. Foster's arms.

"Not to worry." Mrs. Foster laughs. "I'm one of the good guys."

She speaks to him like he's her long-lost grandson, but I'm still too shaken to speak. I can't put into words the relief I feel at not seeing the cops standing in front of me.

"Hello, Zoe." Mrs. Foster glances around the kitchen. "Why are the blinds closed on such a bright morning?"

"Oh, it was too bright," I lie.

"No, it wasn't," Clark cuts in and I cringe inwardly.

Mrs. Foster looks at me, but she says nothing. She knows who the liar is.

When Clark sits back down, I open the blinds again. Then I close the back door.

"We didn't expect you to drop by," I say to Mrs. Foster. "If I knew it was you..." I don't know what more to say, so my voice drifts off.

In the time we have been staying at the cabin, she only dropped by one time.

"I'm sorry. I should have called to let you know." She's wringing her hands in front of her.

Today she's wearing her favorite dress, a purple number with rose petals and pleats. It was the last gift she got from her husband the Christmas before he died. She wears it at least once a week. "I came to check up on you. I baked a pie."

We both look down at her empty hands. She

smiles nervously.

"I guess old age is catching up with me. I forgot it at the house."

"That's all right." I chew a corner of my lip. "I didn't hear your car."

"I came with my bicycle. When my husband was alive, we often rode together."

"That's kind of you."

My knees are still weak, so I sink into a chair after asking Mrs. Foster to sit as well.

She rests her hands in her lap, one over the other. "I do understand that you wanted to spend more time with Clark, but I got the feeling that there might be another reason."

Before I respond to her, I send Clark to the living room to play with the expensive toy train he got from Cole in Disneyland.

When the train sounds make their way to the kitchen, I turn back to Mrs. Foster. She's been kind to me. She deserves to know why I'm keeping Clark away from her even though they both need each other.

"Dear girl, are you okay?" Mrs. Foster lays a hand on top of mine. Her warmth makes me want to reach out and draw her into a hug. "Something is going on with you. You haven't been yourself for quite some time now. You can tell me anything. I'm a good listener."

"You're right," I say after a moment's

silence. "Something is going on." I can't tell her about myself and my past, but I can tell her about her son and what he's been up to. "Your son has been paying me visits."

She slides her hand from mine and closes her eyes. "I had a feeling Ronan had something to do with this." Her face sags. She looks as if she has aged a few years in only a matter of seconds. Her shoulders have curled forward and the bags under her eyes seem to have grown darker and heavier. "In a town like Willow Creek, of course word would get to you. I apologize for not saying anything before about him."

"You didn't have to tell me." As someone who's keeping deeper, darker secrets, I needed to say it.

"The thing is, Ronan does not feel like my son. Yes, I carried him for nine months. Nine months and two weeks to be exact. I brought him into this world, and I raised him, but as soon as he became a teenager, he changed. He became a stranger. He was more attached to his father than he was to me. And when his father died, he took it out on me and his..."

Mrs. Foster lowers her eyes, but I already saw the tears in them.

"His brother?" I murmur.

"Daniel was the light of my life. He tried to

hold things together when everything was falling apart, and Ronan despised him for comforting me."

She stops talking again and we sit in silence for a moment. I don't want to push her. I want to tell her to stop if it hurts too much, but she's not done yet.

"The boys had a complicated relationship since childhood. It got quite violent at times and Ronan usually started the trouble. He spent a lot of time with the wrong crowd. He became violent, even threatening his brother with guns and knives. I was terrified of him, we both were. My worst fears materialized when they went fishing two years ago. Only Ronan returned home."

"Was there an accident?" Tasha said people believe Ronan killed his brother. What if he's innocent? Everyone deserves the benefit of the doubt. If I do, so does Ronan.

"I wanted to believe it was an accident, but Ronan had a gun in his bag that night. Before I could show it to the cops, it disappeared." She inhales sharply. "Daniel had been shot in the head. His body was found floating...floating in—"

"I'm so sorry. If you don't want to talk about it, it's okay." I wipe the tears from my own eyes.

"It's been eating me up inside. Sometimes we have to let things out before they poison us."

I wish I could do the same. I wish I could tell her everything, but I can't trust anyone, not even her. Not yet.

"Zoe, please tell me you're not staying away from me because of Ronan. He's not a part of my life anymore. All he wants is to sell my house and move me into a home."

"That's horrible," I shake my head. "You're perfectly capable of living on your own."

"The truth is, all he really wants is the money he thinks his father left me for him."

I don't know what to say. Instead, I place both palms on the table and stare at my hands.

"I enjoy taking care of little Clark," Mrs. Foster continues. "He makes me feel young again. I would love it if you bring him to the house again. If it's any consolation, Ronan left town yesterday. Said he never wants to see me again. Please, continue your life. Go to work. I wouldn't want you to lose your job because of him."

My heart lifts when I hear news about Ronan's departure. I let out a breath and nod. "I'll bring Clark by tomorrow."

"Excellent." Mrs. Foster pushes back her chair and rises to her feet.

"You're leaving already?" I ask.

She smiles. "I have intruded long enough."

"No, please stay. Have breakfast with us." Since Ronan is not a threat anymore, why not?

She accepts the offer and spends the entire time telling stories of her childhood.

Finally, she leaves, and the day crawls to an end.

In the evening, while Clark is watching TV, I step out onto the porch. I need some space to plan my next move to expose Cole. Then, a note on the porch swing catches my attention, a stone keeping it from being blown away by the wind. The words on the piece of stained paper leave me cold.

Stay away from her or something bad will happen.

Ronan lied to his mother. He's not going anywhere.

CHAPTER 19

Tasha takes Clark to a children's table in a corner of the restaurant and puts coloring pages, puzzles, and books in front of him. He brought his own coloring pencils with him.

Tasha has agreed to let me work half the day because I had to bring Clark with me. It was either that or I couldn't come at all. After Ronan's warning on the porch yesterday, I couldn't risk taking Clark to Mrs. Foster's.

When I called Mrs. Foster about the note, and the change of plans, she sounded hurt, but said she understood.

Tasha walks off and returns with a plate of eggs, toast, sausages, and pancakes. She puts the food in front of a delighted Clark.

"What do you say, Clark?" I remind him.

"Thank you, Tasha." He pushes aside his papers so he can start eating.

"That's all right, little man." Tasha pats him on the head. "If you need anything else, let us know, okay?"

"Thank you," I mouth to her and walk away from the table, but I'll be keeping my eyes on Clark the entire time I'm working. I'll also watch the door in case Ronan shows up.

Tasha pulls me aside. It's a slow morning so we can afford to have a brief chat.

"Zoe, talk to me. I know you're going through something."

I want to, so much it hurts, but what would be the repercussions of doing that? If she believes I committed the murders, she would feel obligated to turn me in. It's hard to know who to trust when you are accused of killing someone. I wish we could be friends, but letting her get close could be dangerous.

"Thank you for caring." My gaze moves to Clark. "You saying that means a lot."

She squeezes my shoulder. "I'll always be here when you're ready to talk."

After leaving her hanging one too many times over the last couple of days, she should have fired me. She doesn't need me. She could hire someone more reliable than I am right now. I know some of the staff complain about me. They have to pick up the slack when I don't show up at work. But Tasha is a good person. She's helping me without prying into my business. For that, I will forever be grateful.

During work, we take turns going to check on Clark or to play a quick game with him.

I'm sitting with Clark at one point, both of us busy completing an ocean puzzle, when Tasha comes to the table with a bright red train.

"Clark, your Mommy said you like trains." She puts it in front of him. "I hope you'll like this one."

"It's mine?" Clark runs his small hand over the back of the brand-new train.

"If you want it to be." Tasha winks at him and walks away. I stand up to follow her.

"You didn't have to do that. You've already done so much for us."

"I would do more if you let me." She pauses. "I understand that you're not ready to share your problems with someone else. But you know what, maybe I understand you more than you think." She starts cleaning a table that has become empty. While she's wiping it down, I stand by the grandfather clock and watch her. What did she mean?

We work side by side in silence until most of the breakfast crowd trickles out and we have time for a short break. Tasha continues the conversation as if we never stopped.

"I was wrong," she says. "I don't know what you're going through. It was wrong of me to imply that I did. I'm sorry about that."

"It's fine," I respond, but I wish she would continue. A part of me is yearning to know her more.

As if reading my mind, she continues, "You might not know this, but I was once a single mother. Jack has not always been in my life."

"Really?" I didn't know that. Whenever he came to the restaurant with the twins, he treated them like his own. I never once suspected he was not their biological father. "I–"

"My late husband died a month after we got married. I was pregnant. We were already struggling financially before his death. When he died, I had nothing to give my kids. The little money he left me went toward the debts he left behind." She sighs. "I struggled for a long time as a single parent. I stayed in a shelter once and worked jobs I hated. Then Jack came along and helped me rescue myself."

"I'm so sorry." Without giving it much thought, I draw her into my arms. She's as surprised by the hug as I am. After an awkward moment, I pull back again, and she smiles.

"The one thing that helped me through rough times was talking about those rough times, especially with someone who cares."

I give her a nod and we stand in silence,

staring at each other. She's waiting for me to open up as well. It doesn't happen. It can't.

When two guests enter the restaurant, I hurry to them, grateful for the distraction. I hope she won't pursue the topic later.

The guests are two women in their twenties. One of them is staring at me in a way that makes me shift with discomfort. She should be flipping through the menu, but instead, her eyes are fixed on my face.

I push back my shoulders and put on my brightest smile. "What can I get you?"

"Oh, sorry." The woman peels her gaze from my face and reaches for the menu. They order pancakes, sausages, and orange juice.

I hurry away from the table, my stomach churning. I'm used to people talking about me when I walk by, whispering behind my back about the eccentric lady living in a cabin in the woods, but this time is different. The woman is looking at me as if she knows me from somewhere and is trying to figure it out.

It's nothing, I tell myself. I want to believe it with all my heart.

When I serve their food, she gives me a sweet smile and thanks me.

"I was wondering," she says before I leave them. "Do I know you? I'm really good with faces and you look really familiar. I feel like we've seen each other before."

"No." A nervous laugh spills from my lips as blood rushes to my brain. "I mean, I don't think so." I force a smile. "Is there anything else I can bring you?"

The two women shake their heads and I hurry off, almost tripping.

"Are you all right?" Tasha asks me at the bar.

"No." It's probably the most honest I've ever been with her. "Can we talk in private?"

Tasha suggests we go to her office, but I don't want to let Clark out of my sight. We take a seat at one of the empty tables.

Her eyes are filled with questions and her hands are clasped on the table. "You can tell me anything."

"No, I can't. I'm sorry. I'm so grateful for everything you've done for me, but I can't work here... not anymore."

The woman with the pancakes might watch the news tonight and see me on TV. If she figures out who I am, she might return with the cops. Even if she doesn't, Lemon has regulars. If they see me often enough, and they keep seeing my face on the news, they will identify me as the woman who's wanted for murder.

"I don't understand. Why?" Tasha narrows her eyes. "Did you find another job?"

I shake my head. The thought of having to

look for another job elsewhere and starting from scratch makes my insides burn with anxiety. Tasha has come to a point where she only wants to help me and she's not pushing to know who I am or where I came from. Another employer might want to know more and they will not be as understanding when I mess up.

As much as I hate it, in the next few days, we might have to leave town, to go to another place where no one knows me. It was a mistake to stay in Willow Creek for this long.

I gaze at Clark and tears fill my eyes. I hate to drag him away again now that he has come to know Willow Creek as home.

"Is it about what I said?" She places a hand on mine. "I hope I didn't overstep. I only wanted to understand you more so I could help better."

"You don't want to know me," I say to her. "I'm too much trouble. Thank you for what you've done. I'll never forget it. And I'm sorry to leave you like this." In spite of myself, I squeeze her hand tight, taking all the comfort I can get.

Before letting us go, Tasha packs up some lunch for us on the house and gives it to me with confusion in her eyes. Five minutes later, Clark and I are back in the car. He's as confused as Tasha was about us leaving so soon.

He doesn't say a word to me all the way to the cabin. I try everything, even ask him to sing with me to the radio. I get nothing back.

"I'm sorry we had to leave, but baby, sometimes parents have to make decisions that kids don't understand."

Still, he says nothing.

The moment the car stops in front of the cabin, Clark gets out and slams the door hard. I watch him stomp toward the front door, clutching his train. He comes to a screeching halt at the porch swing and stares down as if something interesting has caught his attention.

He calls me and I jump out of the car. There's panic in his voice.

"Are you okay, baby?"

"There's blood here." He points to a spot on the floor.

He's right. There's a puddle of blood right in front of the swing.

I bite back a scream before it explodes from my lips.

Pulling myself together, I unlock the door and gently push him inside. "An animal must have injured itself."

I wish I could believe it too. I doubt it though. The blood was put there by someone,

someone who's sending me some kind of warning. Someone dangerous.

CHAPTER 20

❧

"**O**ne more time, Mommy," Clark begs when I finish reading his favorite bedtime story, *The Goose Prince*, a second time. I'm exhausted and ready to drop, but after dragging him out of Lemon today, I owe him.

"One last time." I give in. "Then you have to sleep, okay?"

He gives me a bright smile and curls up next to me on the bed.

While reading, my body is lying next to him, but my mind is drifting to the blood on the porch. I haven't stepped out of the cabin since we saw it, but once Clark is in bed, I need to do something about it. I still can't figure out whether the person who put it there is Cole or Ronan. If Ronan really killed his brother, he's just as dangerous as Cole.

Why would Ronan come back if I'm keeping my distance from his mother, though?

As questions scramble for space inside my

head, I read to Clark on autopilot. I've read the book so many times that I no longer have to read every word.

When I finally reach the end and close the book, I'm relieved, and I hate myself for it. "Time to sleep, little man."

"I'm not a little man. I'm a big boy."

"All right then." I smile and kiss his forehead. "Close those eyes. There's something I need to do outside, then I'll come to bed."

"But I'm scared." He pulls the comforter to his chin, his eyes wide. "Don't go."

"You don't have to be scared, baby. I'm just going outside, and I'll be right back." I continue to lie in bed with him, my arms around his body. He probably senses that danger is close. If only my hugs and kisses could erase his fears. I feel like a fraud telling him not to be scared when I'm terrified as well.

I breathe in several times to try and calm both of us. Finally, his breathing evens out and he places his hands underneath one of his cheeks as he slides into sleep.

I wait a few minutes until he releases the first snore. Then I get out of bed and go to the kitchen. I already have a bucket waiting with water and a rag.

Under the porch light, the blood has dried

into a dark stain. I glance around me, making sure nobody is around. It might be best for me to stay indoors, but as long as there's blood on my porch, I won't be able to sleep. I also don't want Clark to see it again. Or maybe I secretly want to prove to my tormentor that I'm not afraid of him.

Cole draws his strength from other people's weaknesses. Bullies always feel more powerful when they see the fear in their victim's eyes. I may be trembling inside, but I'm going to do my best not to show my fear.

It takes a while to wash away the blood. Once I'm done, part of the dark wood is pale from being scrubbed so hard. There's a can of varnish in the cabin. When I get the chance, I'll cover up the scar so Mrs. Foster won't become upset about it.

I throw a look over my shoulder again and push to my feet. My heart is slamming against the inside of my chest as I stare into the dark trees, but my face is stoic and my normally hunched shoulders are pushed back.

I make it back into the cabin without being attacked. I lock and bolt the door and all the windows. The cabin is old and frail. If someone wants to break in, they can easily do so, but I'll be able to hear them.

I take a broom and a knife to the bedroom

and lean the broom against the wall on my side of the bed. The knife goes under my pillow, wrapped in a kitchen towel. I'll get rid of it before Clark wakes up and starts asking questions.

I still can't sleep. My heart refuses to settle, even after several calming breaths.

I get out of bed again and head to the kitchen, knife in hand. I can't leave it in bed with Clark.

Since I don't have anxiety meds, I boil myself a cup of chamomile tea. After a few sips, I feel the urge to step out of the cabin again. The walls are closing in on me.

Before I know it, I'm standing on the porch again.

My fingers are still tight around the knife in case I need to protect myself.

The crickets are especially loud tonight, and their chirps mixed with the sound of the babbling creek is more calming than any tea. I lower myself onto the side of the porch swing furthest away from where the bloodstains were, place the tips of my toes on the wood and rock back and forth.

That's when I see it, a bundle covered with a muslin kitchen towel. It's tucked in one corner of the porch, behind a dead potted plant. I get up from the swing and brace myself for whatever I'm about to find.

When I lift the cloth, I gag.

It's a dead squirrel with eyes wide open, its little body lifeless and stiff. The dried blood on its coat tells me what I need to know. If it weren't for the fact that it was covered up, I would have told myself that it got injured and hopped onto the porch to protect itself from scavengers.

Forgetting how to be brave, I rush back into the cabin and slam the door shut, my back pressed against it.

I slide to the floor, my arms around my trembling legs.

I feel cold and I'm shaking all over. I cannot go to bed, not this way. Clark would notice me shaking next to him.

One of the men hunting me is out there, probably right now in the bushes, watching the cabin, waiting for the perfect time to attack.

He's a cold-blooded killer. What would stop him from hurting Clark? Losing my son would be a fate worse than death itself.

Too weak to get up, I crawl to the couch and cry myself to sleep.

When I open my eyes again, it's 4:00 a.m. As much as I hate going out there again and seeing the dead squirrel, I need to get rid of it. Clark loves animals. He'd be devastated to find a dead squirrel on the porch.

Since we arrived in Willow Creek, Clark has been begging me to get him a dog. It disappoints him when I refuse, but I can't afford a pet. Being on the run with a small child is hard enough. Right now, though, I'm wishing we had a dog to warn us when danger is close by.

I take a garbage bag and hold my breath as I drop the squirrel into it. The rotting smell makes my stomach turn.

I'm about to throw the bag into the outside bin when a glint catches my eye. It's the blade of a small knife with a bloody tip.

It has to be the weapon my tormentor used to kill the squirrel. He knew I would find it. He wanted me to. I drop the squirrel inside and throw up next to the bin.

"Are you okay, Mommy?" My world spins when I turn to find Clark standing on the porch. Vomit is still trickling down my chin and my eyes are wild with horror.

I quickly slam the lid onto the trash can and wipe the vomit from my chin with the back of my hand.

I take his arm and hurry him to the door. "Let's go inside."

"What is it?" he asks, his voice still sleepy.

"Mom is not feeling that well." This time it's

the truth.

I don't want Clark to be out here again. I don't want him to be in the line of sight of a murderer.

If it's Cole, he's giving me a clear message. He killed before and he can do it again.

I can't let that happen.

CHAPTER 21

❧

My mind is yelling for me to run, to take Clark and the few belongings we have and get out of Willow Creek. But I can't be impulsive. I can't run blindly without knowing where I'm going, and my mind is too disturbed to come up with a plan.

It's clear now that no matter where I go or how far we run, Cole will find us eventually.

Leaving the cabin, our only home, could be a mistake. We have nowhere else to go.

The best thing to do right now is to stay put and calm down enough to come up with a plan that makes sense, instead of running blindly toward some other town where more danger could be awaiting us.

We have stayed indoors for three days with nothing out of the ordinary happening, but we're running out of food. We have no choice but to get out there again and stock up.

Clark is overjoyed when I tell him about our

trip to the grocery store. Everything goes smoothly. I stuff a bag with canned foods, rice and pasta, and anything with a long shelf life.

We're at the cash register when Clark decides to be difficult. He's angry because I refuse to buy him a superhero toy.

We can't waste the little money we have, not when I don't have a job to bring in more.

I place my hand on his head, trying to calm him, to prevent him from throwing a tantrum. He has been doing that a lot lately as the stress of being cooped up inside the cabin has gotten to him. I'm struggling as well.

He knows I'm not well. He knows I'm afraid. On more than one occasion, he woke up in the middle of the night to find me looking out the window, or saw me jump when he walked into the room. I'm stressing him out. If only I knew what to do about it.

"How about I get you this instead." I reach for a less expensive toy race car.

People are watching. We need to get out as soon as possible.

At first, he protests, then he throws up his arms in defeat. "Fine," he mumbles and folds his arms. "Can I get the other toy next time?"

"Maybe." Maybe one day I'll be able to buy him what he wants, but right now, I cannot spend fifty dollars on a toy. I toss the new toy into the cart and wheel it forward to pay, satisfied that we'll have enough food to last us a while.

The plan is to hide out until I can decide where to go from here, how to keep us safe, now that my photo is all over the news and papers.

Out of the corner of my eye, I try not to stare at the newspaper on the stand with a small photo of me in one corner of the cover. When I was a kid, I wondered how it would feel to be famous, to grace the covers of magazines. Now that I'm in the limelight, I know that it's definitely not what it's cut out to be.

I pay quickly and rush Clark back to the car, but as soon as I shut his door, the feeling of being watched arrests me. My skin prickles as I freeze in place, not daring to turn around, afraid of what I might see.

Then I take a deep breath, hold it, let it go, then I look.

My feelings were right, Ronan is still in town. My body is tight with tension as our eyes meet from across the parking lot. He's inside his pickup truck, staring blatantly at me, his eyes digging daggers into my skin.

I want to charge toward him and demand he stay away from us, but it's better to keep a distance. I only hope that he does not come to the cabin again. I haven't gone to his mother's house, so he has no reason to want to harm me.

Unless he's found a different one.

I take another breath and hold it. My eyes are still on him as I slide behind the wheel. My palms are slick against the old leather of the steering wheel.

Ronan doesn't have to worry. I only need a few days to come up with a plan, then I'll leave Willow Creek behind to start over someplace else, maybe a big city that will enable us to merge with the crowds.

Clark says something from the backseat, but I cannot hear his words. Through the rushing in my ears, his voice sounds distant.

I watch as Ronan drives away, his truck disappearing around the corner.

I let out the breath I was holding and rest my forehead on the steering wheel.

"Are you okay, Mommy?" Clark asks and I swallow hard before I turn to look at him.

"Mommy is just tired, baby."

"Is it because you don't sleep?" he asks. "You went to the window again. I saw you."

Oh, my God, what am I doing to my son? It's not only me waking up in the middle of the night, I'm waking him as well. "I'm sorry that I woke you," I say.

"It's okay, Mommy. Don't feel bad. You

should drink warm milk."

He has no idea that I feel like I'm the worst mother in the world.

"That's a good idea. Maybe I will." I ignore the tears threatening to fall.

Without another word, I pull out of the parking lot and drive back to the cabin, glancing in the rearview mirror every few seconds to make sure Ronan is not behind us. I don't see his truck.

But what about Cole? Is he out there hiding in plain sight? Or does he have someone doing his dirty work for him?

My phone rings. It's her. She already called several times today.

I don't pick up Mrs. Foster's call. Our phone conversations are always about the same thing. She's still desperate to see Clark. When she called last night, she begged me to take him to her.

I reminded her again that I'm terrified that Ronan will harm us if we don't keep our distance.

She assured me again that he has left town.

Maybe she really believes it. It could be that he had left town, after leaving me the note, and decided to come back to haunt me. Now that I have seen him with my own eyes, I need to do what's right for us. I can't speak to Mrs. Foster yet, but there's someone else I need to call.

On our way to the cabin, we drop by a public phone. I park as close to it as possible because Clark refuses to get out while playing with his new race car.

With my eye on my car, I dial the number I found in the Fort Haven online directory.

When the phone starts ringing, nervous butterflies erupt in my belly. I haven't spoken to Denise for years.

After she stopped working at the hotel, I tried to call her several times, but she never answered or returned my calls. Not long after, her number went out of service, so I gave up and went on with my life.

But now, she might be the person with the ammunition I need to fight Cole. I need to know why she left the hotel. It could be the same reason the other employees left as well.

Since Denise's cell number still doesn't exist, I'm calling her mother's house phone. I knew Denise said at the time that she lived with her. She could have moved out, of course, but her mother might be able to give me her new contact details.

The phone rings five times with no answer. I'm about to hang up when someone picks up.

"Hello?" The woman has a raspy, tired voice. "Who is this?"

"I'm sorry to disturb you. I'm an old friend of Denise. I'm unable to reach her on her cell. Is she in?"

Silence.

"What do you want from my daughter?" She sounds both curious and annoyed.

I rub the back of my neck. "We haven't spoken for a long time and I just wanted to get in touch."

"I'm sorry." She cuts me off. "You can't speak to my daughter."

My heart sinks. As I suspected, she moved out. It has been years, after all. Maybe she's married and had another kid, in addition to the son she had when I knew her.

But she had said at the time that her mother suffered from epilepsy, and was also dependent on a wheelchair to get around, so she needed constant care. All the same, maybe she's better now and Denise was able to start her own life.

"Would you mind giving me her new cell phone number? The one I have no longer exists."

"That's because she doesn't either. Denise is dead."

"She's what?" My throat tightens. "How? When?" I sink against the dirty glass of the cubicle. My eyes are blurry as I stare at my car outside.

"A year and four months." Her voice is barely audible. "She was a good girl."

"Yes," I assure her. "Yes, she was. How did she... How did she die?"

I don't want to put the woman through any more pain, but I need to know. I had not known Denise for long, but I had really liked her. While the other ladies at the hotel were distant and cold toward me, Denise had made me feel welcome.

"The cops said she killed herself, but I don't believe it. My baby would never do that."

"No," I murmur, my fingertips touching my parted lips. "No, she wouldn't."

CHAPTER 22

❦

Clark is eating his fries and roasted chicken while I move my food around the plate. The news about Denise's death has hit me really hard, and I'm too preoccupied to eat.

I don't understand. If she died a year and four months ago, her death has to have happened around the time Brett was diagnosed with cancer.

Why would she kill herself? She was struggling financially and often told me how hard it was to care for both her mother and her three-year-old, but she was optimistic that things would get better. She was one of the most positive people I knew.

She was the kind of person who spent her free time reading motivational books and had affirmations plastered to the inside of her staff locker. Even though, like me, she didn't finish school, she was determined to create a better life for herself and her child. Working as a maid was only temporary. Her dream was to start her own wire-wrapped jewelry business. She showed me a few pieces. She was talented.

Now it's all over. She died with her dream inside of her.

I don't understand how that could have happened. I don't want to.

After telling me about what happened to Denise, her mother was so distraught that she couldn't speak anymore. I didn't get any of the answers I needed.

I wipe away the tears before Clark sees them. I'm tired of him asking me if I'm okay. I'm tired of stealing his childhood innocence, making him grow up before his time because he feels he has to take care of me.

I need to get my life together before I destroy him completely.

When Clark is playing in the living room after lunch, I go in there with my notepad.

Something about Denise's death doesn't seem right. Like her mother, I don't believe she committed suicide.

A disturbing thought crawls into my mind. What if in some twisted way, Cole had something to do with it? What if Denise didn't commit suicide and she was murdered? But that doesn't make sense either.

I massage my temples, ignoring the

headache creeping up on me. I need a clear head, to figure out how much of a monster Cole really is.

If it was really him who had killed Denise, what motive did he have? She no longer worked at the hotel.

There's only one explanation. Maybe she had something on him. It was no secret that she disliked the man, everyone did.

I need to speak to her mother again. I hate to bring back the memories of her daughter, and I would definitely hate for her to think that someone hurt her, but what if I could help bring her some kind of closure?

The idea of going out there again gives me stomach cramps. I need to use my phone. Denise's mother didn't know who I was, so she wouldn't contact the cops.

I remind myself that prepaid phones are hard to trace. When I bought mine secondhand, I didn't need to offer much personal information. For the cops to trace me, they would also need to know what name I'm using. If they did, they would have revealed my new identity to the press already.

I bring out the number and call again. She doesn't pick up, so I try again ten minutes later.

I'm surprised when she recognizes my voice. "What do you want this time?"

"Mrs. Sanchez, I'm so sorry to remind you of what happened to your daughter. I can only imagine how hard it must be."

"No, dear," she says. "You can't. No one can imagine the pain a mother feels after losing a child. No one will understand how deep that pain is." When she utters the last words, she sounds as if she's talking to herself and no longer to me.

I swallow a sob. "She was my friend and I don't believe that she did it. I don't believe she took her own life. She loved her child, and she loved you. She would never willingly leave you."

"But what if she did it and I refuse to accept it because it hurts too much? My daughter was in pain," Mrs. Sanchez blows her nose. "I don't want to think that she did it, but since she started working at that hotel, she changed."

"In what way?"

"She had the most beautiful smile and she stopped showing it. She cried every night. We needed the money, but I told her to leave that job. When she did, I still didn't get her back. My happy Denise was gone forever. I lost her even before she died."

I knew Denise was not happy at the Black Oyster, but I had no idea how deep her unhappiness was.

"Did she explain why she was so unhappy?" I ask gently. "Did someone hurt her?"

"I need to go. I've said enough." Mrs. Sanchez's voice has hardened.

"Mrs. Sanchez," I am almost begging. "If somebody hurt your daughter, you need to tell someone. We don't want the same thing to happen to anyone else."

The phone goes dead.

She told me enough. I'm certain now that Cole is responsible. It's time for me to speak up. I don't have evidence to support my accusations, but I'm hoping that my words could at least plant a seed into the hearts of those that can provide justice.

Before I lose my courage, I change the sim card in my phone, replacing it with a different one. Then I make an anonymous call to the police department in Fort Haven. I use the non-emergency number to make it less likely they'll trace the call.

"I would like to report Mr. Cole Wilton for the sexual assault of his employees at the Black Oyster Hotel." I beg them to start an investigation.

"Do you have proof to back up these claims?" the policeman asks in an urgent tone.

"I know Cole Wilton is sexually molesting his employees because he did the same to me.

He threatened to kill me if I told anyone." I sniff as memories flood back. "If you don't do something about it, I'm going to the press."

"Could you tell us your name?"

"No." I hang up quickly. I replace the sim card with the old one in case Denise's mother or Mrs. Foster want to reach me.

Burying my head into my hands, I weep as I relive every second of that painful night. I should have spoken up before now. Maybe I would have stopped the chain of events that followed, the deaths. But I didn't, and now it feels like it's too late.

For years I have lived with my secret, not even telling Brett because I knew it would destroy him. I didn't want to risk losing him over it, because I loved him so much. At the same time, I hated myself every day for keeping such a secret from him.

I probably dug my own grave by calling the cops. But it's time. Cole needs to pay for what he did, especially now that it's no longer just about me. He lives in a luxury suite at the Black Oyster. God only knows what he's up to in there when he's not working. He's a monster and the world needs to know.

I meant what I said about contacting the press, too, if the police don't take action. I cannot prove that Cole killed his own son and the housekeeper, but maybe a sexual harassment investigation will help uncover the truth.

The doorbell rings while Clark and I are watching TV after dinner. Panicking, I draw him closer to me. "Go to the room and put on your pajamas, and don't come out until I say so."

When Clark is in the room, I tiptoe to the front door and peer through the peephole. My head snaps back.

It's Ronan.

"I know you're in there," he barks in a slurred voice. Something hard hits the door and I jump back as I hear glass shattering. Probably an empty beer bottle.

I didn't hear his truck. He must have parked a distance away and walked. "Get the hell out of my cabin," he continues when I don't respond.

I cover my hand with my mouth as a piece of the puzzle slides into place. That's it. That's why he's been after me all this time. Before he went to prison, he probably lived in the cabin, and now his mother is renting it to me.

"I don't know what you're hiding, woman, but your eyes have a story to tell. You're hiding something and I will figure you out. I'm a criminal and I can sniff out another criminal from miles away. A little bird told me you're running from the law, that's why you're hiding out here in the woods."

While I'm struggling to figure out what to do, the distant sound of police sirens cuts through the silence around me.

He already knows who I am. He called the cops on me.

It's game over.

Clark appears in the living room. I feel him before I see him. I turn around and run to him, clutching him to my body. "Mommy loves you. I love you so much." I press my lips on top of his head. "Please forgive me."

"Did you do something bad, Mommy?"

"I don't know," I say, then I bite hard into my bottom lip.

I wait inside the cabin as the sirens grow louder. I'm afraid to open the door. These might be the last moments I have with my son.

And then, raised voices, followed by a gunshot.

Someone starts shouting. It's Ronan's voice.

Confusion clouds my mind. The only thing I can do is hold on tighter to Clark, waiting for the police to break down the door.

But they don't. After what seems like forever, there's only a knock.

"Miss, this is the police, are you all right in there?" It's a woman's voice.

I blink away tears. "Yes." My voice is too low for the policewoman to hear me. I try again. "I'm really fine."

The policewoman orders me to open the door.

I'm terrified, but I do as I'm told, still clutching on to Clark's hand. She sounds more concerned than angry, but if I don't let her in, she might use force.

The woman looks from me to Clark. "Are you or your son hurt?"

I shake my head as my eyes zoom past her shoulders to see Ronan's figure inside the police car. They didn't come to arrest me; they came for him. I don't know what for, but the relief I feel to see him being taken away is enormous.

After asking me a couple of questions, they drive away. I'm still free, but for how long? Ronan could very well tell them what he knows about me in return for lighter punishment.

CHAPTER 23

～

They didn't come for me. It was Ronan they wanted.

But they were close, close enough to shake me.

I turn around and see Clark's damp, red eyes. I can tell he was terrified by everything that had just happened, but he also looks very sleepy.

I draw him to me and squeeze him. "You don't have to be scared. I won't let anything happen to you." Clark tightens his arms around me. We hold each other for a long time, then I release him. I place my hands on both sides of his face and give him a watery smile. "Mommy will always be here."

He nods, then he walks to the bedroom and closes the door.

I sink to the floor. I got away this time, but for how long? How long until they return to get me?

Blood drains from my face at the sound of a car nearing the house. They're back already. Ronan must have figured out who I am and told them on the way to the station. Now they have returned before I can run.

Everything is happening too fast. My mind hasn't even gotten a chance to recover from the initial shock.

I'm shaking on the floor when the doorbell rings.

"Open the door, Zoe." It's Mrs. Foster, not the police. What is she doing at the cabin at 8:00 p.m.? She normally heads to bed around 7:00.

The moment I get to my feet, a wave of dizziness washes over me, getting worse with each step toward the door.

Before I can open it, Clark runs into the room, calling out Mrs. Foster's name. The joy in his voice, the laughter in his eyes make my heart hurt. He opens the door before I can and Mrs. Foster steps in. The wrinkles on her face look like they have deepened even more, the bags under her eyes darker.

She hugs Clark for longer than usual, putting her chin on the top of his head, closing her eyes. Then she lets go and puts both hands on his shoulders.

"I need you to go to bed now. It's late. I'm

sorry if I woke you."

"The police were here," Clark blurts out. "They took the bad man away."

"Is that so?" Mrs. Foster glances at me, then back at Clark. "I need to have a quick word with your mother. Be a good boy and go to bed."

Clark's face falls. "Can I visit you tomorrow?"

I pull myself together and step in to rescue Mrs. Foster. "Clark, it's time for bed. Come on." I take his hand and walk him out of the room. Mrs. Foster waits in the living room until I've tucked him in.

I find her sitting on the couch, her back straight, hands clasped in her lap. She doesn't look at me when I enter, staring straight ahead at the blank TV screen.

I sit next to her. She still doesn't look at me.

"Ronan was here," I say quickly because if she doesn't know already, she deserves to know that her son is still in town, that he's still stalking me. She has to understand why we're keeping a distance.

"I'm aware of that." Her chin hits her chest. "He told me he was headed here."

"He came to see you before he—?"

"No, he came to threaten me. Since I refused to give him money for drugs and alcohol, he demanded I kick you out of the cabin. He threatened to harm you. He had a gun. I called the police."

"Thank you." It must have been hard for her to call the cops on her own son. "It was his cabin, wasn't it?" I ask.

"It was the family cabin. He only thought it belonged to him. He thinks everything belongs to him." She pauses, taking a deep breath. "Zoe, I'm so sorry, but I have to ask you to leave."

"I don't understand." Confusion washes over me as I look at the side view of the woman who has been so kind to me over the last months. I knew I would have to leave at some point, but I thought it would be on my terms.

"I think you do." Her voice is low as she finally looks at me. "Meghan Wilton, that's your name, right? When I gave you a place to stay, you didn't tell me you are wanted for murder."

I can't find it in me to deny it. Her eyes tell me she knows everything. I've lied to her long enough. I don't even know how to talk myself out of this situation, what more lies to feed her.

"I'm not one to watch a lot of TV, but lately, I've had a lot of time on my hands. I saw a photo of you on the news. You look very different...like someone else. But the woman

on TV has this same heart-shaped birthmark."
She places a hand on my shoulder and her
thumb brushes the birthmark on my
collarbone. "In one of the photos you wore a
strapless evening gown. That's how I saw it."

I normally hide the mark when I go out,
wearing clothes and makeup that cover it up,
but she must have seen it the day she showed
up with her bike. I had been wearing a
spaghetti-strap top.

When I don't speak, she removes her hand
from my shoulder and continues. "You change
your hair and eye color every month. I knew
there was something strange about it. I
didn't…" Her voice trails off. "They said the
fugitive woman also had a four-year-old son
who must be five now."

I open my lips to speak, but no words come
out. "It's not what you think. I loved my
husband. He was sick and–"

"You don't have to explain anything to me.
I came to tell you that I need you to leave by
tomorrow night. I have come to be very fond
of your son. And for his sake, I won't notify
the police. But I need you to go. The sooner
the better. Leave the key under the mat."

"Thank you." I blink away tears. "Thank you
for everything. But it's not what you think. I
didn't… I'm not a–"

Mrs. Foster raises a hand and gets to her feet. "Like I said, I don't want to know anything more. Take your boy and run. Murderers are not welcome in my home or in my life." Tears are glistening on her cheeks.

She feels betrayed, but if I had told her sooner, she would probably have made the same decision she's making now. But maybe she would have been hurt less because she wouldn't have gotten close to Clark.

Even though Clark is in bed, she asks me for permission to say goodbye to him, and I ask her to follow me to the room. He's already sleeping.

She stares at him for a long time, then kisses his forehead. In that moment, he opens his eyes. She simply smiles at him and says, "sweet dreams."

I can tell he knows it's goodbye.

As soon as Mrs. Foster leaves, I tell Clark we'll be leaving the cabin and he starts crying. My attempts to comfort him fail as he pushes me away and locks himself in the bathroom.

We are about to lose the cabin, and now I feel as though I'm losing both my son and my sanity. He's all I have, and I cannot afford for him to slip through my fingers.

Right now, though, I need to respect his space. I have already put him through a lot. He thought we had found a home. He had come to see Mrs. Foster as the grandmother he never had. And now he just found out he might never see her again. It's too much for a little boy to deal with.

But sometimes life can be cruel and you either crumble or you do what you have to do. You survive.

I give Clark the time he needs. I wait in the living room, in the same spot on the couch where Mrs. Foster had been sitting.

The one advantage about renting the cabin is that we didn't have to bring many of our own possessions. It came furnished already. Everything we own can fit into two small bags.

When Clark finally comes out of the bathroom, he joins me on the couch.

I hold him in silence. He knows something major is going to change, and I know he understands.

"Are you ready for another adventure?" I ask, rubbing my hands together. "We're leaving in the morning."

"Okay," he says, but his voice is empty of emotion. Without asking me where we are going next, he helps me pack.

Before we go to bed, I write Mrs. Foster a letter to thank her for all she's done. On the other side of the page, Clark draws a picture of a little boy carrying a toy train.

CHAPTER 24

Lying next to Clark, I consider our options. Do we move to another small town or a big city? Wherever we go, I don't think we will find as good a hiding place as the cabin. I doubt we will find another Mrs. Foster waiting for us at our next destination.

The desire to be free is so strong. It hurts almost physically not to be able to go out and do what normal people do without looking over my shoulder.

As long as I'm not free, Clark won't be either. His freedom is tied to mine. He won't have the luxury of a normal life like other kids. He will be scarred by every bad decision I make. The consequences will suffocate both of us.

Will he blame me one day for the choices I'm making right now?

Before I fall asleep, I decide that we will hide out in Rogersville for now. It's only an hour away and we had stayed in a motel there for a few days before choosing to settle in Willow Creek.

Having decided, I finally fall asleep, too exhausted to even dream.

In the morning, I'm in the living room going through the notes I've been writing when another car pulls up in front of the cabin.

I peer out the window. It's not the police. It's Tasha. Surprised to see her, I open the door before she rings the bell and wakes Clark.

"Hi." I hesitate before letting her come inside. It's her first time visiting me at the cabin.

"I'm sorry, did I wake you?" she asks. "I won't be long."

"No, it's fine. Clark is still asleep, though." I'm quiet until she sits herself down in the living room without me offering. "I'm surprised to see you," I say.

She pinches the skin at her throat, I can't tell whether she's doing it because she's nervous. "Zoe, I'm worried about you. After the way you left the restaurant the other day, I needed to make sure that you're fine."

I feel suddenly cold. What if Mrs. Foster told her about me? I want to say something, but I don't know what that would be, so I keep my mouth shut.

"So, this is where you live." She takes in the living room, her gaze resting on the broken armchair by the window.

I nod. "But not for long. We're going away."

"For good?" Her eyes widen. "You can't do that." She gets to her feet. "Clark is so happy here. I know how moving around can affect a child. My kids hated being moved around."

"I don't have a choice." I run a jerky hand through my hair. "We need to go...away."

"Did Mrs. Foster ask you to leave?"

When I don't respond, she sighs. "Why don't you come and stay with us until you figure out what to do next? We have a guest house on the grounds. You and Clark can stay there."

"I don't want to get you in trouble." As soon as the words leave my mouth, I realize the mistake. Now she will know that I'm running from the law.

She's only quiet for a moment, then she squeezes my arm. "Don't worry about that. I'd like to think we are friends. Friends are there for each other."

She's right about that, but we can't be friends. She doesn't know the real me. I want it to stay that way. I still haven't recovered from the look of betrayal in Mrs. Foster's eyes. I wouldn't be able to stand Tasha looking at me like that, too.

"Tasha, you have no idea how much your offer means to me, but I can't accept it."

"All right, then." She sounds disappointed. "Then take this, okay?" She reaches into her purse and hands me an envelope. "It's your payment for this month and a little extra from me. Hopefully it'll cover you while you find a new place to stay."

I know it's rude, but I open the envelope and look at the cash inside. "Why are you doing this?" I ask when I see that there's an extra two hundred dollars.

"Because when I was in a tough situation, many people helped me out along the way. I'm paying it forward. I care about you and your son, and I want you to be safe. But please, let me know where you're going. You have my number, call me when you need anything, or if you change your mind about coming to stay with us."

"Thank you, Tasha. Thank you so much." I want to refuse the extra money, to give it back, but I can't. Every bit counts, and I'm touched deeply by her generosity. I can refuse to hide in her home, but I can't refuse the money.

Before she leaves, she hugs me tight. When she lets go, there are tears in both our eyes.

"Take care of yourself," she whispers. "And

if you need anything, call me. Anything at all."

I promise that I will, but I probably won't. But I have her number just in case.

As soon as she leaves, Clark comes out of the room, looking confused as he looks around him.

"Are we staying here again?" His face brightens up. "Can we visit Mrs. Foster again?"

"No, baby. We're still leaving."

Even though I made a decision about leaving Willow Creek, it's still too terrifying to go to another town just yet. I'll find a decent motel in Willow Creek for now, one that's far from the people who have come to know us.

Before we leave, I cut Clark's hair, then I cut mine as well into a pixie style, shorter than I've ever worn it before. This time, I choose a jet-black color.

New look, new start. Hopefully, things won't go horribly wrong.

CHAPTER 25

I slide the coins into the motel snack machine and Clark chooses corn chips for his treat. I feel like a terrible mother for feeding him junk food, but I need him to be happy. If that means buying him snacks, that's what I'll do.

I paid for our three-night stay at the Midnight Motel in cash. There are only ten rooms in the motel and two are occupied. The owner hands me the key and we walk to our room.

One thing I hate about most motels is that one doesn't have to go through reception in order to get to the rooms. Anyone can simply show up at your door.

I slide the key into the lock and turn it. The door squeaks when I open it.

In the beginning, Clark used to get excited every time we entered a new place. It felt like a new adventure. This time, he doesn't even look at the room. Instead, he walks blindly to a rickety chair by the window and sits down, then he pushes his hand into the bag of chips.

He hasn't said much during our drive to the motel. He's still hurting. I wish I had the power to erase his pain.

Before we left the cabin, we both stood outside and said a proper goodbye to it, thanking it for sheltering us during the time we spent there. I told Clark we are like nomads, never staying in one place for too long because we crave adventure. He simply shrugged his shoulders and got into the car.

How long can I still fool him into believing this is how normal people live? How long until he starts asking the most difficult questions?

I'm about to draw the curtains to let in the sunshine, but my hands drop to my sides again. Anyone outside would easily be able to see inside when they walk past our room.

When we were driving, I didn't feel as though we were being followed. For the first time in a while, I didn't, and still don't, feel Cole's presence.

Maybe I was wrong all along, maybe all those things that were happening at the cabin, the cupcake, the squirrel, and the blood. Maybe they were all Ronan trying to chase us out of the cabin and Cole had nothing to do with it.

But I still have to remain alert in case I got

it wrong.

"It's too dark, Mommy." Clark looks up from his chips. "Can you open the curtains?"

"Let's keep them closed for a little while, okay?"

"No," he demands. "I want to read my book."

"All right." I open the heavier curtain just enough to brighten the room. The sheer curtain underneath stays in place.

Satisfied, Clark moves over to the bed, puts his chips next to him, and opens the fairytale book he had been flipping through in the car.

He's pretending that everything is normal, and it hurts me. I hate that I can't offer him more than this, at least not right now.

When my phone rings inside my purse, I hold my breath. The only two people who normally call are Mrs. Foster and Tasha.

The caller ID is hidden. I don't answer without knowing who the caller is.

I stare at the phone until it stops ringing and beeps to signal that the person has left a message.

I listen to it right away.

"Hello, this is Mandy Sanchez, Denise's mother. Hi, please call me back." She sounds like she's in a hurry.

At first, I berate myself for forgetting to hide

my caller ID when I called her, then I realize it was probably a good thing, otherwise she wouldn't have my number. I never expected her to call me.

While Clark is still leafing through his book, I sneak outside to return the call.

"The police came to my house," Mandy says as soon as she hears my voice. "They wanted to speak to me."

"About Denise?"

"They said they received anonymous calls about the harassment of employees at the hotel where my Denise worked. They wanted to know if Denise said anything to me before she died."

Had my call to the Fort Haven police worked? "What did you tell them?"

"I told them the truth. That man, Cole Wilton, hurt my child. He hurt her."

I want to ask her to tell me exactly what he did to Denise, but I already know.

"It was brave of you. I'm so sorry for what happened to her." I believe now more than ever that Denise didn't kill herself, but what if the police don't find evidence to prove she was murdered?

"Who are you?" Mandy asks. Her question takes me by surprise. Last time she didn't seem interested in my name.

"Denise's friend," I repeat what I told her last time.

"Can you help me?" she asks. "Can you help get justice for my daughter? She didn't deserve to die that way. They say she jumped out of the window of our apartment, but I don't believe it."

The image of my friend lying dead on a pavement burns a hole in my heart. "I don't know if I can help. I'll try." Tears are clogging my throat now and Clark is at the door, eyeing me suspiciously.

"Please, she was all I had. I dream about her every night. Someone needs to pay for what happened to her."

"I know," I say. "They will."

I don't know what I can do from a distance. It's complicated trying to bring Cole to justice without exposing myself.

"Thank you," she says. "I'll tell the police everything. I'll look for her journals and give them to the police."

"That's good." My heart lightens. "That's a good idea."

"My Denise used to love journaling," she continues. "She said it helped free her mind. I hope her words will lead the police in the right direction."

When I end the call, I'm starting to feel

confident that Cole is going to be punished for at least one of the crimes he committed. And after that, I will work hard to reveal the others.

Feeling hopeful, I gather my son into my arms and hold him until he gets squirmy and starts to push me away. "Mommy, I can't move."

After I let him go, I make us tomato sandwiches and we eat in front of the TV without switching it on. I don't want to make the mistake of falling asleep with the TV on and waking up to find him seeing my face on the news. Even though Clark begs to watch cartoons, the TV stays off.

After lunch, I read him his favorite books until he grows drowsy and falls asleep. I'm about to close the curtains again when I catch sight of a police car parked in front of the motel.

In a panic, I check to see if the door is closed. The motel owner must have recognized me and called them to come and get me.

Either way, I'm stuck. I'm cornered. I glance at my son. I've failed him. I've destroyed his life.

The police car remains in the parking lot for an hour, but no one gets inside it. I keep expecting the police to knock on the door, but they don't.

The urge to use the bathroom forces me to walk away from the window. When I return, the car is gone.

The best thing I can do right now is to stay put and hope for a miracle.

Staying in motels doesn't feel safe.

For a split second, I consider calling Tasha to ask if the offer to stay in her guest house still stands. I remind myself that I might be putting her in danger by doing that. Plus, what if her husband is not on board?

It's definitely a bad idea, one that could hurt too many people.

I lie next to Clark and pull him into my arms, protecting him the only way I can.

CHAPTER 26
Six Years Ago

⤬

The day before my wedding to Brett, I stood in the entrance to the wedding banquet hall.

Everything was ready for the reception.

I wanted to say it was perfect, but life had taught me that nothing ever is.

I couldn't tell whether the butterflies in my stomach were brought on by excitement that I was about to marry the man of my dreams, or the fear that something would go wrong.

I chose to focus only on what could go right. Brett and I were about to start the rest of our lives together. He had promised me the world. I promised him the same. After three months of dating, I felt like we'd known each other all our lives.

Fragrant champagne roses spilled from every corner of the room, mingling with the expensive lace and silk. Some of them were also wrapped around the chandelier above the monogrammed dance floor.

I flinched when someone slid their arms around my middle. Then I smelled his warm, woodsy cologne before I turned to face him.

"Good morning, wife." He kissed the side of my neck.

"You can't call me that quite yet, Mr. Wilton," I said, leaning in for a kiss. "Just a few more hours left."

"I can't wait." He leaned his forehead against mine.

"Are you imagining us dancing on the dance floor?"

"Oh, yes." I smiled.

I enjoyed our moment, then pulled away, my expression serious. "I'm sorry your father won't be here."

His father had made it clear that he did not support our union and would not attend.

He did not believe in marriage and he found it appalling that his son was choosing to marry a former maid. He even threatened to disown Brett if he went ahead with the wedding. When we first got to know each other, Brett told me that his father loved to control his life, but he put his foot down when it came to choosing whether, and who, to marry.

Cole decided to go out of town during the

festivities so he would not witness us becoming husband and wife.

It gave me some sense of comfort to know he wouldn't be there. I could not stand the man. I found it hard to breathe in his presence, and Brett was stiff and uncomfortable when his father was around.

Cole was overbearing and barked orders at Brett as though he were a child.

"I prefer not to have him around," Brett said. He looked more relaxed than he usually was. I loved that carefree side of him.

"Still, he's your father and it must hurt."

"It doesn't," Brett said and pulled away. His eyes glistened. He couldn't hide his pain from me.

He placed both hands on my cheeks and kissed me again. "The honeymoon suite is ready for you. You're spending the night here at the hotel."

"I am?" I raised an eyebrow.

"Of course. My girl deserves to sleep in comfort before her wedding day. I want you to be well rested. I don't want you to ever sleep in that shabby apartment of yours again."

I swatted his arm. "Stop calling my apartment shabby."

He was right. The small one-bedroom apartment I lived in was far from the luxury of a suite at the Black Oyster, but when I came to Fort Haven from New Jersey, in search of a fresh start, it was all I could afford.

After I started dating Brett, he insisted I move in with him, but people were already gossiping that I was with him for his money. I didn't want to give them even more ammunition. Even when he proposed, I refused to move into his house, which was owned by his father.

The only time I was prepared to move in with him was as his wife. He finally respected my decision.

But the night before our wedding day, it would definitely be nice to sleep in a comfortable suite, where my wedding dress would not be squashed up in a tiny closet.

My life felt like a fairy tale coming to life.

After accepting his offer, he personally drove me to my apartment to get my things. Then he dropped me off at the hotel and asked the staff to help me settle in.

My former coworkers hardly said a word to me. They did what they had to do and left. I got the feeling that they saw my marrying Brett as a betrayal of some sort. They no longer knew how to communicate with me or act around me. I understood where they were coming from, but that didn't make it hurt any less.

In spite of what they all believed, I was with Brett purely for love. I was not the kind of woman to marry a man for his money. The moment I met him, just after his father hired me, it was love at first sight. It did take a few weeks for us to start dating, though, because I found it hard to get past the fact that he was my boss.

He kept seeking me out in the hotel, asking if everything was going well. It was something he didn't do with the other housekeepers, at least not that I noticed.

Eventually, he asked me to dinner. When his father found out, he was furious, and I was ashamed. I was not surprised when Cole called me a piece of trash and fired me on the spot, right there in the restaurant. He thought that would be the end of it.

Brett apologized and promised that his father would never come between us again.

I soon learned that Cole always had his way, and the way he treated his own son was despicable. He degraded him and made him look weak even in front of the employees at the hotel.

After I was fired, Brett continued to come and see me. He also helped me get a job working in a restaurant that belonged to one of his friends. At first, he offered me money to help me out, but I refused it. I preferred to earn my own money. I didn't want to rely financially on a man who wasn't my husband yet.

After a few weeks of seeing each other secretly, he proposed. I said yes without thinking about the possible consequences. Foolishly, I thought maybe now that I was going to be his wife, his father would respect our relationship.

Brett arranged a dinner with the three of us so we could announce our engagement. Cole did not show up, so he had to find out over the phone. That's when he came to the restaurant to punch his son in the face, breaking his nose.

"Marriage is for weak men," he said between clenched teeth. "Marry that woman and you will regret it."

Despite his father's threats, Brett refused to give me up.

Now we were getting married, and even though I was excited, I was nervous as well. His father was the fly in the ointment. Maybe it was best that he refused to come to the wedding.

Standing in the honeymoon suite, I decided not to think about my future father-in-law. I didn't want him to ruin everything for us.

Surrounded by the sweet scent of the red roses in vases around the room, I lowered my wedding dress onto the couch and threw myself onto the four-poster bed, erupting into giddy laughter.

I had just finished having a long bubble bath when someone knocked on the door. I was not seeing Brett again that day, so it had to be one of the staff.

I slid into a fluffy bathrobe and swung the door open.

I stumbled back when I saw my future father-in-law standing in front of me. He was normally impeccably dressed in one of his black suits and gray shirts, but this time, the suit jacket was gone and his tie was loose. I had never seen him anything other than impeccably dressed before, and I had thought he was out of town.

My first thought was that he had changed his mind and decided to be by his son's side, after all. Maybe he had come to apologize to me for all the names he had called me. But his expression wasn't one of remorse.

I tightened my bathrobe cord and forced a smile. "Cole, I thought you were out of town."

"You would like it that way, wouldn't you?" he said. "It would be the perfect opportunity for you to trap my son in your web."

"I love your son, Mr. Wilton." I pushed back my shoulders to appear confident. "And I'm not marrying him for his money."

"So, you're telling me that if I disowned him today, you would still marry him? Do you know that everything he has belongs to me? If I take it all away, he would have nothing."

My eyes were heating up when I responded. "Of course. I would marry him any day because I love him. But I'm guessing that's something you don't know much about."

The grin that spread across his face left a chill down my spine. "Are you going to allow me to stand out here, or will you let me into a room that belongs to me?"

I let him in, and it turned out to be one of the worst mistakes of my life.

The moment the door closed behind us, he planted a hand on my chest and shoved me back. I could not stop myself from falling to the floor. When I tried to get up, he lunged over me.

"Looks like someone needs to teach you a lesson," he drawled.

"Let me go," I shouted, but his hands were now tight on my wrists and his body pressed me down.

"Do you know why I hired you in the first place?" he whispered into my ear, his breath warm against my earlobe. "It was not because I thought you could do the job. It was because I wanted to see how your body would look in a tight little uniform."

As panic swept through me, I tried to free myself from him, but he pressed harder until my back hurt.

"Let me go," I shouted again, but then he clamped his hand across my mouth.

"You're not going anywhere. And Brett can't come and save you. I arranged a long meeting for him. I own you, just like I own him." He blew a liquor-soaked breath into my face. "He's nothing, you know. He's not the man you think he is. He's a little boy, but you're too blind to see it, aren't you?"

His words pierced through me. I tried to scream, but his hand was so tight against my mouth that no sound came out.

"Like I said, everything Brett owns belongs to me. That includes you."

With that, he put his other hand on my throat and choked me until I was too weak to fight him. Then he went ahead and damaged me the night before my wedding, breaking every perfect moment I was ever going to have with Brett.

Before he left, he put a gun to my head and told me if I ever said a word to anyone, he would kill me.

I believed him and buried the secret deep inside my heart.

CHAPTER 27

❧

I never expected it to happen so soon or so dramatically. In fact, I didn't expect it to happen at all.

I was trying to get back to sleep when my phone beeped gently with a message from Denise's mother.

Switch on the news.
—Mandy

Thankfully, Clark is sleeping like a stone and didn't even budge when I found the remote in the dark and switched on the TV. The volume is low, and my ears strain to hear every word.

I watch the TV screen in awe, as it bathes the room in color.

Cole Wilton's face is all over the news on almost all the news channels. Across the top of the screen, in bold type, the headline reads:

Breaking News: The Downfall of

Businessman Cole Wilton

Now my mouth is hanging open as I watch the man I feared the most being led out of the Black Oyster in handcuffs. A monster has been captured. On the screen, he's trying to fight the police off, saying something I can't hear, but the cops have a good handle on him.

I'm almost weak with satisfaction as I watch him being robbed off his power. I guess nothing lasts forever. Deep, dark secrets have a way of coming out into the open. Cole's are currently in the spotlight, and they are uglier than I ever could have imagined.

A male reporter with a gelled lock flopping over his forehead throws a glance behind him and then back at the camera. His eyes are shining with excitement. He is clearly pleased to have landed a story that is sure to go viral.

Early this morning, hotel mogul Cole Wilton was arrested for the sexual harassment of dozens of his housekeeping staff. You can see him here behind me in handcuffs, being led out of his Fort Haven Black Oyster luxury hotel, where he also resides.

We've been told that an anonymous caller tipped off Fort Haven police to a pattern of abuse at the Black Oyster, which kicked off the investigation. Since then, at least ten women, all maids at the hotel, came forward to share devastating stories of sexual abuse, bribery, and sometimes death threats.

We will keep you updated as this explosive story unfolds.

I cover my mouth with my hand. I knew there had to be other women out there, but I didn't expect there to be so many.

Swallowing a sob, I wrap my arms around my legs. I return to that night, the night he broke me, the night he poisoned my marriage, the night that led to me standing in front of my future husband the next day a shell of my former self. The vows I exchanged with Brett that day no longer held meaning because I was keeping a devastating secret from him. Cole had not come to the wedding. He had left the hotel, and possibly town, after it happened. But he was still there. When I said, "I do", it was Cole's face I saw in my mind. When I danced with my new husband at the reception, I kept thinking I saw him among the guests.

After the wedding, I struggled to connect with Brett. He couldn't understand why I was pulling away from him, why I wouldn't let him touch me on our wedding night, not knowing that I was hiding the emotional scars and the physical bruises his father left on my body. Not wanting to lose Brett, the only man I ever loved, I faked my way through our marriage. I learned to pretend I was happy when I wasn't, until it felt real.

It was hard. The nightmares came almost every night. My anxiety went through the roof, and I had to start taking pills to manage it. I was terrified every night that I would talk in my sleep and Brett would find out what I had been hiding from him.

There were many times I tried to tell him, but I didn't think he would survive learning of his father's ultimate betrayal. Cole reminded me every chance he got that if I said a word to anyone, he would kill me. After what he did to me, I didn't want to underestimate him, and I didn't want to lose Brett.

Now, for the first time in a long time, I feel lighter. I don't know how long it will last. I don't know whether Cole will remain behind bars. He's a powerful man, and he can hire the best lawyers. But now that the world knows that he's not squeaky clean, my hope is that while the cops investigate, they will find evidence to prove that he's not only a rapist, but also a murderer.

I won't rely on the law to figure it out themselves. I'll do what I can from my end. I'll make another anonymous call in the morning to sow the next seeds.

Now that Cole has been arrested, I have

more faith in Fort Haven's new chief of police. Cole was not able to bribe him. I read in a report that the man was ruthless. That's what Cole needs, someone as ruthless as he is.

Clark groans and turns over.

I quickly switch off the TV in case he opens his eyes and sees Cole being arrested.

But a few minutes pass and he doesn't wake up. I switch on the TV again. I need to see more.

Several of the maids at the Black Oyster are now being interviewed. I don't know most of them because they're probably new, replacing those who had left after Cole damaged them.

Some of the women are crying, some hugging each other.

"He told me that he only hired me because he wanted to see if I was a natural redhead," a gorgeous redhead says to the camera. "At the time I was grateful because I didn't have any experience for the job. I didn't know I was going to work for a monster."

"Why didn't you tell anyone?" a female reporter asks.

"I was scared of him. He said he would kill me. And he offered me money. My mother is in a nursing home. I couldn't say no."

The camera switches to an older woman with short gray hair. She's in a wheelchair and the reporter goes down to her level to speak to her.

Who is she? She's not one of the maids. Cole only hired young women.

When she finally speaks, I smile in spite of myself. It's Denise's mother. She's going public, and I cannot be prouder.

"That man is a monster. He hurt my baby. My Denise used to be a maid at the hotel from hell. He ruined her, and then he threw her out. But that wasn't enough for him. He had to kill her too."

The reporter is as shocked as the people around her. "What makes you say that, Mrs. Sanchez?" he asks. "Are you accusing Mr. Wilton of murder?"

Mandy's chest rises and falls, then she gazes straight into the camera. "The police said she jumped from the window, but I didn't believe it. I still don't. Cole Wilton did it. He killed my baby. My daughter would never take her own life. She had a son she loved very much. She would never leave him willingly."

"Mrs. Gonzales, do you realize the enormity of this accusation?"

"It's not an accusation," Mandy's voice rises as people watch her in horror. "It's the truth. That man deserves to rot in prison for the rest of his life. When he fired my daughter, he threatened that if she ever said anything, he would kill her. He kept that promise."

"Why didn't she go to the police about the death threats?"

I had asked Mandy to speak up, but I never expected her to accuse Cole of murder. She's doing the work for me.

"The day she said she would go to the police, she ended up dead."

When Mandy is done talking, and the topic changes to something else, I switch off the TV and lie on the bed. My head is spinning as I stare into the dark. As much as I'm glad Cole is being brought to justice, I'm horrified about all the things he has done. With so many accusations against him, it will be hard for the authorities to let him go. They have to deny him bail, surely.

I want to sleep, but I can no longer do so. I'm both exhilarated and frightened. It's a relief to know that Cole is being held responsible for something, but he's a very wealthy man. If they make the mistake of allowing him to be released on bail, he could run. Nothing would stop him from changing his identity and living another life in some other country, where he might even continue to fulfil his sick desires.

In the morning, I bundle Clark into the car and take him out to buy breakfast, so we can eat it at a park. At the checkout counter in the grocery store, my gaze moves to the magazine and newspaper display stand.

Cole's face is on the cover of several papers. To distract Clark from seeing Cole, I give him some money and tell him to move ahead because he's a big boy and can pay for our food. He grins up at me and takes a few steps forward.

I'm about to reach for one of the papers when I spot another with a small photo of Cole in a corner of the cover, next to that of another man. Brett Wilton. The headline makes me want to throw up.

Father and deceased son were sexually abusing employees for years.

CHAPTER 28

Tears plop onto the article on the floor of the bathroom. I don't want to believe the words.

He was my husband, the man I loved from the moment I saw him, the father of my son. He couldn't also be a monster like his father. He couldn't have done all the horrible things I'm reading about in the papers that are spread around me on the bathroom floor.

From the other side of the locked door, I can hear the sound of Clark playing a game on my phone. I have the TV remote with me, so he can't switch it on.

I thought it was over. I thought Cole would finally pay for his crimes. I never expected to be hit with a bullet that would scar me even further.

Brett would never have done the things he's being accused of. And yet, it's all there in black and white. Several women came forward to accuse him of sexually molesting them on several occasions in various rooms of the hotel.

The can of worms that I opened has also revealed other truths that bring a sour taste to my mouth. It didn't stop with Cole and Brett.

Multiple allegations also say that Cole Wilton and his son, Brett Wilton, were offering maids to other powerful men who stayed at the Fort Haven hotel, to do with as they pleased during their stay.

Several more reports claim that the Black Oyster was not just a hotel. It was a secret brothel, a retreat for monsters like Cole and Brett Wilton.

As much as I'm desperate to bury my head in the sand, the truth is unfolding inside my head as well. Pieces of the puzzle are clicking into place.

I knew it. Deep down I saw the signs, but I didn't question anything. What normal person would have believed such horrors were going on right under their nose?

I should have known that Cole wouldn't stop at raping his son's future wife. After what he did to me, what would have stopped him from doing the same to other women?

But Brett? I knew he lived his life doing everything to prove to his father that he was a man, that he was not the coward his father thought he was. He was desperate for his father's approval. How far did he go to prove himself?

The worst kind of betrayal eats at my insides when I replay some of the words I read. They will forever be burned in my mind.

I wouldn't have believed a word anyone said about my husband, but one of the women was quoted as saying she was raped by Brett seven years ago.

I got pregnant with his child. When I told him, he fired me and forced me to get rid of my baby. His father showed up at the clinic and offered me money to disappear. He said he would kill me if I returned.

It doesn't matter that most of the women who accused Brett of raping them mentioned dates before I married Brett. Maybe he fell in love with me and stopped. It doesn't matter. It doesn't erase the sins he had committed. He had been leading a double life that he hid from me.

The tears are flowing hot and fast, dripping down my chin and into my neck. My head hurts. My entire body hurts. I can't think. I can't move. I don't know how I will be able to take care of my son when I'm such a mess.

How will I be able to hide my pain from him.

"Mommy, are you crying?" he asks from the door. I didn't know I was that loud.

I gather up the papers and stuff them into a plastic bag, which I hide in the cupboard under the sink. Then I take a breath and open the door. I pull Clark into my arms. "I'm so sorry, baby," I mutter into his hair. "Mommy is just so sad."

"But daddy is sleeping in heaven. He doesn't have pain."

"I know." I cry harder, my body shaking. "I'll be fine. We will be fine."

I don't know whether I'll ever be okay again. Too much has happened. How will I ever recover from this? It feels like my life is over, and I feel terrible because I have someone else to take care of.

I have to pull myself together for Clark. He's all that matters now.

I hate Brett for what he did, and I'm even glad he got cancer. I'm not a bad person. I never want anyone to hurt, but he hurt me and so many others. Then again, he would have suffered even more in prison than in death. I wish he could look me in the eye right now and see the pain he has caused me.

How could he be so evil? How could he stoop to his father's level? How could he hurt those poor women?

During our marriage, he spent a lot of time at the hotel, sometimes through the night because of what I thought was some emergency. I should have known that instead of being in his office, he was probably sleeping with the employees.

The first thing I noticed when I started working at the hotel was that all the housekeeping staff were stunning. Even though I had been told often that I was pretty, I felt like a frump next to most of the women around me.

Now it all makes sense. Now I understand why Cole was furious about his son dating and then marrying me.

He hired me to be shared between the two of them, but Brett wanted me for himself. That's why Cole did it. He wanted to put a mark on me, to own me before Brett did.

The sick bastard.

I spend the rest of the day waiting for the night, when Clark would sleep again, so I can grieve in peace. As soon as he starts snoring, I head back to the bathroom. I wish I could open the front door and start running, to scream out my frustrations at the top of my lungs, but I can't leave Clark. I'm stuck in this place, in my little bubble of misery that's getting smaller and more suffocating with every breath I take.

I clutch my chest and bend over the sink, watching my tears dripping into the bowl, darkening the grime that's so deeply ingrained into the ceramic that it cannot be washed away.

I allow myself to cry because that's all I can do. While my son sleeps in the other room, I'm crumpled onto the dirty tile floor, my arms wrapped around myself, my nails digging into the flesh of my arms.

I thought I knew pain. I thought I knew disappointment, but what I'm experiencing is something so all-consuming that it steals my breath right out of my chest, leaving me with only a gaping hole in the center of my heart.

"Brett," I whisper through my tears as snot slips into my mouth. "How could you? How could you do that to me... to us?"

I feel guilty for only crying for me when there were so many others who were hurt, some even more than me. They were all used and thrown away like rags. They probably thought I was one of the lucky ones, or that I knew what was happening and didn't care. Brett wanted more than my body. I don't doubt that he loved me. I don't doubt that he wanted to spend the rest of his life with me, but his father had so much control over him. I hated it when Cole called his son a coward, but now I think he was right. Brett was a coward not to have stood up to his father.

One of the women said they were glad that

Brett died. They said he was violent and cruel and treated them like pieces of crap.

That was not the man I knew. The man I knew was gentle and loving. But I guess I never really knew him. Was he a rapist or was he a loving husband and father? Now he's gone and I can never ask him that question. But Cole is alive and he will pay for his crimes. With any luck, so will the other men who were also involved.

Some of the male guests who came to the hotel had been identified, and the police were already making arrests. Several of them were from out of town. It seemed they only came to Fort Haven to take advantage of what was being offered at the Black Oyster Hotel. Then they went back to their lives, maybe even to their wives and kids, leaving behind shattered hearts and bruised bodies.

I want to walk out there and add my story to all the others. I want to tell the police exactly what Cole did to me, but unlike those women, I'm also labeled as a murderer.

I have to trust that whatever Cole is hiding will come to the surface.

My phone beeps with a text message. I drag myself to my feet and grab it from where it lies next to the sink.

It's Denise's mother again.

Thank you, she says. *Thank you for encouraging me to speak up. I hope he dies in prison.*

That's my hope as well. I want Cole to pay for both his sins, and also Brett's.

CHAPTER 29

❧

This morning, I woke up determined to fight. Other victims out there are fighting, coming forward with their stories, however painful. They are facing their worst nightmares, and here I am hiding.

Yes, I have more to lose. I could end up behind bars, but the desire to speak up and share my truth burns inside me like hot lava.

I had planned on calling the cops yesterday, but hearing what Brett did completely threw me off. But I'm doing it now. I've switched the sim cards, and I'm speaking to a Fort Haven police officer. After telling her that I worked at the hotel and Cole also raped me, I move on to the topic of the murders.

"Cole Wilton is capable of more than rape." My voice is lowered so Clark doesn't hear the conversation from the room. To be on the safe side, I've also turned on the shower. "I think he killed his son, Brett Wilton, and the housekeeper."

"Ma'am, can you tell me what makes you come to that conclusion?"

"I just know it. Please investigate him."

"Ma'am, I need you to tell me your name." It's the second time she's asking me since we started talking.

"My name is not important. What's important is that you start an investigation into Cole Wilton. He killed his son, his son's housekeeper, and possibly Denise Sanchez."

I don't have the evidence, but I trust my gut. I was right before when I suspected he sexually abused his employees. I could never have imagined the scope of it, but my feelings did not let me down. Now that I've done my part, the police should stop searching for me and turn their full attention on Cole.

"Ma'am, we cannot go on without proof to support your claims," the police officer continues.

"Find the proof." I hang up.

I want to tell them more, but I can't without revealing who I am.

I thought long and hard last night about all the pieces that were missing. The night Brett died, I definitely heard a sound. Cole had to have been in the house. I don't know what he was doing there, but he was there.

I'm not done yet. I'm determined to prove he was the murderer, but I can only go to the cops and show my face if I have concrete proof.

Bracing myself, I call Marjorie again. The last time we talked, she would only talk about what a good person Cole is. A lot has happened since then. She could have changed her mind. My job is to convince her to tell the truth.

She picks up on the first ring. "What do you want?" she asks. The strain in her voice tells me things have certainly changed since our last conversation. She no longer sounds excited to be interviewed.

"Ma'am, last time we spoke you told me that you entered the house with Cole Wilton. Do you still stand by it?"

"So, it's you," she says with a sigh. "I already told you everything that happened."

"So you say, but our paper prides itself on its accuracy, so you'll understand that I need to follow up, considering the circumstances." I pause. "I'm sure you've heard that Cole Wilton is accused of raping several women in his hotel."

Marjorie goes quiet, but her heavy breathing is very audible. I start to worry that she will hang up on me like she did last time.

"All lies," she finally blurts out. "Everything

that's been told about him is nothing but lies. There's no proof."

"But there is," I shoot back. "The women he raped, the victims, have come forward to tell their stories."

"He's a very wealthy man. I wouldn't be surprised if they only want money from him."

"Like you?" I ask without flinching. "We did a little research on you, Miss Smith. We've heard claims that you have been needing a hip replacement surgery for quite some time, but until recently, you couldn't afford it. Yet now our sources say you have had the surgery. May I ask where that sudden windfall came from?" I watched a lot of videos of her being interviewed. Not in a single one of them did she have the cane she had been using for years because of her bad hip.

"That's my business," she shouts.

"Was it Cole Wilton?" I keep pushing. I'm still surprised she's not hanging up. Maybe at some deep level she wants to tell me the truth. "Did he bribe you into keeping the truth from the police? Do you realize that by hiding his secrets, you are hurting innocent people and actually hindering the police from doing their job?"

She doesn't respond, so I continue, piling on the guilt. "You are standing by a man who did terrible things to innocent women. He used them like sex slaves."

"Those women could be prostitutes and they lied!" I hit a nerve because her voice is wavering. "I prefer to give people the benefit of the doubt."

I let out a sarcastic laugh. "Like you gave Meghan Wilton the benefit of the doubt? What if it was your child? What if you had a daughter that worked in that hotel and was raped by Cole Wilton? If you're hiding something to protect that man, now is the time to come out so he can be put to justice."

"Mind your own business. I don't want to be featured in your paper." When she hangs up, my blood is pumping, my face hot with anger. It's not the end. Even though she refused to admit the truth, she still might. I never thought Denise's mother would go to the cops, and yet she did. All I needed to do was give her a push.

The only thing I can do right now is cross my fingers and hope for the best. There's not much else I can do from a distance.

Marjorie is the backup I need for the cops to believe me. What I told them over the phone will become even more real if she comes forward as well and tells the truth. If there's one thing I've learned, it's that the truth will come out eventually.

Like the truth about Brett.

I'm still hurting when I think about the things he did, how he blinded me into thinking he was a good man even though he was doing his father's dirty business.

I'm about to open the door and get back to Clark, when I remember something. The day of our anniversary, Brett received a call from his father. He was informed that two housekeepers had quit their jobs at the hotel. He insisted that he had to handle the situation. Come to think of it, every time someone quit, it was usually he or his father who handled it. They probably went to pay off the women or threaten them with death. Or they eliminated them completely. What if Brett wasn't only a rapist but was involved in eliminating the women who threatened to expose them? What if he was involved in killing Denise?

The thought makes me slump forward as a dagger of pain shoots through me. I turn back from the door and throw up in the toilet.

Images are floating inside my mind, images of Cole and Brett sitting in one of their offices or suites, discussing which women were becoming too much trouble and should be fired. Did they also sit around a table to discuss which women were beautiful enough to hire?

I wipe my mouth and rinse it, then I stand tall. I can't let this break me. Life is filled with nasty surprises, and I have to be ready for them. I have to be ready to fight back this time. I've always been a victim in my life, but that's over now. Anger is my fuel. Anger at Cole and anger at the man I used to call my husband.

"You will get through this," I whisper to myself in the mirror, then I return to the room to eat lunch with Clark and pretend everything is all right when it's far from it.

CHAPTER 30

❧

We're eating breakfast in a booth at the Oak Diner instead of inside our motel room.

The low "yummy" noises Clark is making while finishing up his pancakes and bacon warm my heart. Taking him out for breakfast was a good idea.

Now that Cole is in police custody, the police are probably occupied with his case instead of searching for a woman who hasn't been seen in a year. I now feel safer going outside more often.

I had to get Clark out of the motel room. After five days indoors, the walls were starting to close in on us and Clark was becoming increasingly irritable.

Even though I don't think I'm the police's highest priority right now, I'm still glad the restaurant is not packed. There only a handful of guests around the scratched tables.

We still need to be careful to keep our identity a secret.

When we entered the restaurant, I was still able to breathe, but now that my eyes are glued on the small propped-up TV, I have suddenly forgotten how to.

Thankfully, Clark is sitting with his back to the TV, otherwise he would have seen his grandfather's face on the news. I'm still surprised at how I managed to shield him for this long. Sooner or later, he's going to face the truth of how damaged his family really is.

But not yet. Not today.

The other customers are staring at the TV as well, some shaking their heads when they take in the breaking news update scrolling at the bottom of the screen.

After being released on bail, Cole Wilton has disappeared.

"Mommy, I want more breakfast." Clark holds up his dull metal fork.

I stare at him, my head spinning. Then I shake myself into action and jump up from my chair.

"We need to leave." It's a good thing we're seated not too far from the door. We'll be able to make a quick escape before Clark sees Cole's face and shouts out that it's his grandfather. That would certainly get the other diners' attention and our cover would be blown.

"I don't want to go," Clark whines, biting on a piece of crunchy bacon. "I want to finish my bacon."

"Sweetie, that's your last piece. You can eat it on the way to the car." I hate that, yet again, I'm about to drag him out of a restaurant without an explanation, but I have no choice.

While he continues to chew his food, ignoring my request, I reach into my purse for money. I drop a twenty-dollar bill next to the vase of fake red roses.

Feeling guilty, but also losing my patience, I reach for Clark's arm. He yanks it from my grip and his eyes flash at me. An invisible hand closes around my throat because for a split second, his eyes remind me of his grandfather's.

I jolt back a little before moving forward again. He *is* my son. He has Brett's and Cole's blood, but he will never turn out like them. I will make sure of it.

"Why do we always have to go early?" Clark juts out his bottom lip.

"I'm sorry, but sometimes we have to do things we don't want to do. And we stayed long enough for you to finish your food." I search my brain for something to comfort him. "We can play some more games at the motel."

"I hate the motel. It's stupid."

"Don't say that." I reach for his arm again and pull him out of his chair, still looking at the TV out of the corner of my eye. He continues to fight me off, but I'm determined to get us out of the place.

"Clark, please, do what Mommy is telling you. I'll explain later." I won't be able to explain the situation to him, but there's nothing else I can find to say. I feel as though I have been repeating myself over and over again, making him the same dry excuses, feeding him the same old lies, withholding information.

"I hate you." He pushes away from me, but he doesn't sit back down. Instead, he storms out of the restaurant.

I'm reeling with both hurt and relief. It's amazing how crushing a few simple words can be.

From a distance, I see the waitress approaching our table. I give her a small wave and she nods after she sees the money on the table.

During the drive back to the motel, Clark refuses to speak to me. It kills me inside, but I understand.

He barely speaks for the rest of the day, and at bedtime, he goes to bed without a fight. He's hurting and I don't know how to help him heal without telling him the truth.

As soon as he's asleep, I switch on the TV and slide to the edge of the bed, blocking his view in case he opens his eyes.

Cole really did escape and there are suspicions going around that he might have skipped the country. I wouldn't be surprised. His whole empire is crashing down because of his own sins. He doesn't have anything holding him back in the US, and he certainly has the resources to hide in another country.

I bury my hand in my hair when the reporter repeats all the things Cole and Brett have done to their employees over the years. Every word is like a knife to my heart.

I bite my bottom lip, trying to breathe, to manage the emotions raging through me. How could I have been so wrong about my husband?

My mind takes me back to something he had said a few days after we got engaged, the night Cole punched him in front of me. He revealed to me that as a kid, one of his father's favorite forms of punishment was to lock him in a cupboard, sometimes for hours. He also loved to scare him. Brett was terrified of snakes, and that fear started when his father brought a snake into the house one day and put it in a glass case in Brett's room. Apparently, he wanted him to toughen up, to be a man. He was only thirteen, and the snake spent the night in his bedroom. When he cried, his father called him weak and pulled out his belt to punish him for that weakness.

No wonder Brett was obedient to his father even in his adult years. He still lived with the fear of his father and did everything he demanded of him, just like he had done as a child. He also told me that when he turned eighteen, his father's gift to him was a visit to a strip club. At the time, I was disgusted and didn't want to hear more. I wish I had dug for more information, maybe he would have revealed the secrets they kept. But what could I have done? Like Brett, I was terrified of Cole. How could I have known that he groomed his son into becoming a rapist like him?

"I'm sorry, Mommy," Clark's sleepy voice makes me jump. "Sorry I was bad to you."

I switch the TV off and crawl back into bed next to him.

"You're not bad, Superboy." I kiss him on his warm cheek. "I'm sorry for taking you out of the restaurant before you finished eating."

Honestly, we could have stayed a little longer. I had panicked and the only thing on my mind was to flee. It's an automatic reaction that has kept us safe for this long. Every time I see Cole's face, every muscle in my body prepares to run.

This time, I guess I needed to be alone, too, to process the news without Clark watching me from across the table. Hiding my pain from him is one of the hardest things I have ever done.

"I love you, Mommy," he whispers and draws closer to me, burying his face in my chest as he used to do when he was a baby.

"I love you much more." I close my eyes and rest my chin on the top of his head. "Forever together?" I ask.

"Forever and ever," he whispers.

Warmth spreads through my chest, soothing some of the cracks on my heart. But more cracks are still appearing.

I wish I could watch TV again, to follow the story, but there's really not much to see anymore. It will be a while before they find Cole. If they ever do.

At the back of my tortured mind, I wonder what I will tell Clark one day when he finally grows up enough to understand the crimes committed by both his father and grandfather. What if the fear that he might inherit their behavior becomes stronger?

I squeeze my eyes shut to force the thought from my mind. I refuse to believe it. Clark will be a good man because I will be the one raising him, not those monsters.

I choose to believe that one day the truth of what really happened to Brett and Janella will be revealed and Clark and I can finally live normal lives. If it doesn't happen, I might not be able to repair the damage our situation has already caused him.

CHAPTER 31

It's been almost a week and Cole still hasn't been found.

It's definitely enough time for him to ensure he's never found again.

My hope is dwindling by the minute. He could be anywhere, doing God knows what, possibly continuing his dark deeds. His rotten obsession is not something he will be able to shake off.

I'm not the only person disappointed that the cops have not found him. The residents of Fort Haven are so furious that they are taking matters into their own hands.

Our motel room is dark, but the orange flames on the screen are splashing it with a warm glow.

Fort Haven's Black Oyster Hotel is burning to the ground. Firefighters surround the place, but the building that had once boasted power and luxury is turning to ashes faster than it can be rescued.

In some way, I feel a great sense of relief. The place held too many terrible memories, and it's now being destroyed, set on fire by protesters who had camped outside for days.

People are angry that one of their own has shattered the safe image of Fort Haven. Parents are afraid for their children. The residents are going to extremes to demand that something like this never happens again.

I can't help but wonder what Marjorie thinks now. Does she still believe Cole is innocent? Is she still determined to hold on to the lies he asked her to tell? She had said in an interview that only a guilty person would run. That's exactly what Cole is doing.

I tried to call her yesterday, to try and convince her to go to the police, to tell them what Cole paid her to do for him, but she hung up the moment she heard my voice.

The story about the murders has not been mentioned yet. I'm wondering whether the police are trying to keep it quiet to keep Cole from running harder.

Wherever he is, he's probably watching the news. It brings me satisfaction to imagine the pain on his face as he watches everything he has built literally turn to ashes. Of course, he has hotels in other states around the country, but the hotel in Fort Haven was dear to his heart.

Or maybe he doesn't even care. He could be watching the news with a sick grin on his face, possibly glad that the fire is destroying whatever evidence was left.

When my phone vibrates next to me, I flinch. No one has called me for quite some time.

I consider not picking up, but when I glance at the screen, I recognize the number.

It's Tasha. Why is she calling after all this time, and so late?

The phone keeps vibrating. If I'm not careful, the sound will wake Clark.

I switch off the TV and tiptoe into the bathroom with it glued to my ear.

"Zoe," Tasha says. Her kind voice wraps me in a silken cocoon of warmth. I didn't realize how much I missed being in touch with another adult, someone who cares. I kept hoping Mrs. Foster would call to find out how we're doing, maybe ask to speak to Clark, but she never did.

"I'm sorry for calling late. I didn't want to disturb you, but there's something I think you should know." She goes quiet and continues in a low voice. "Mrs. Foster has passed away...heart attack."

A ball of shock hits my core. "Wh… what?" My mouth is so dry the word comes out distorted. "When did it happen?"

"Yesterday morning. She was found by a neighbor. No one knows how long she has been dead."

The idea that Mrs. Foster died all alone in her house tears at my insides. I start to cry, holding onto the phone, afraid to let go, desperate for whatever comfort Tasha can offer me from a distance.

"I feel responsible." Tears are drowning my words. "It's my fault."

"Why would you say that? She died of a heart attack. No one is responsible for that."

I want to tell her she's wrong, that finding out my secret probably killed her. Losing Clark could have been more painful for her than I ever imagined.

I lean against the cool tiled wall. "How about–how about Ronan?"

"From what I heard, he's still in prison. It doesn't seem as if he'll come out anytime soon. Apparently, he committed quite a few crimes in the short time he was out. Mrs. Foster had no other family members, so we will be arranging her funeral. I was wondering if… Would you like to come?"

I can't answer the question. What do I tell

her? The funeral will probably be filled with people who will recognize me from when I lived in the cabin. Her neighbors–who saw me dropping off Clark at her house–will probably be there.

But Mrs. Foster was like family to me and Clark. Will I ever be able to forgive myself if I don't go? She had done so much for us. Plus, wouldn't it be selfish of me to deny Clark the opportunity to say a proper goodbye to the woman who had loved him like her own grandson?

"Okay," I whisper. Since Cole's arrest, my face hasn't been plastered all over the television and papers. Maybe I can get away with this. "When is the funeral?" I ask.

"A week from Saturday. At the Willow Creek Memorial Cemetery at 2:00 p.m. I'm sure Mrs. Foster would have wanted to see you there. She really liked you and she was devastated when you left."

It's clear that Mrs. Foster did not tell her what she discovered about me, otherwise, Tasha would probably turn her back on me too.

"And Zoe, it will be really nice to see you again."

I swallow a sob. "It will be nice to see you too."

When I hang up, my hands are shaking, and I sink down to the floor. My fingertips pressed against my eyes, I remember the old woman who had been kind to me from the moment I met her, the woman I had betrayed because I withheld the truth from her.

It's too painful for me to think I could have contributed to her death. I have to hang on to what Tasha said to prevent the guilt from eating me alive. I convince myself that she was probably more devastated about Ronan than about us. He was her son, her real family. We were just strangers passing through her life.

I told Tasha that I looked forward to seeing her, but she won't get to see me close up. Clark and I won't get close enough for the other mourners to see us. It's safer that way. If by any chance Ronan is released from prison to attend his mother's funeral, who knows what he might do?

He had already told me to stay away. He could be the one who made his mother suspicious of me. I can't be sure that Mrs. Foster didn't reveal my real identity to him, even by mistake.

But I do owe it to Mrs. Foster to show up, to give our final goodbye, to thank her silently for everything she's done for us, for the protection she gave us for all those months.

It will be hard not to be able to speak to Tasha at the funeral. For her to call me and tell me about Mrs. Foster's death means she cares more than I want her to. I did everything to push her away, and yet she kept coming back.

I never wanted to go back there again, but life has a way of pulling the carpet right from underneath my feet and forcing me in a direction I don't want to go.

I weep for Mrs. Foster as if she was my mother and not someone I'd only known for a few months. In my mind, I can see her eyes brightening up whenever Clark ran into her arms.

I remember the sound of her voice, warm and kind before she knew the truth about us. I also remember how she had sounded the day she asked us to leave, so cold and broken. It hurts that her last words to me were drenched in disappointment and pain.

I sneak out of the bathroom and get back into bed. As soon as he feels me beside him, Clark moves closer and curls his little body into mine, but he doesn't wake up.

"I'm sorry," I whisper into the night. I don't know what I'm sorry for or who I'm apologizing to. Is it to Mrs. Foster? Is it to Clark? Is it to myself? Is it to all three?

Either way, the words come out and they

hold so much meaning. I certainly need to forgive myself for the mistakes I've made, the biggest one of them being that I entered Brett's life.

But there's one reason why I don't regret it completely. My son was worth all the pain.

CHAPTER 32

◦◦◦

I've made an effort to camouflage myself as best I can. I have my dark glasses on, a cap pulled over my forehead, and dark clothes that don't scream "look at me". Sometimes I wonder if the sunglasses and cap make me look more suspicious. But being outside with nothing to hide behind makes me nervous.

Even though Clark looks much different than a year ago, I still asked him to wear a baseball cap. At first, he refused to put it on, but then I reminded him that we're still playing the undercover spies game. He took the cap but refused the sunglasses.

Telling him that Mrs. Foster had died was hard. Strangely, he seemed more upset about her death than Brett's. After hearing the news, he withdrew into himself for a full hour, only speaking when I spoke to him.

Finally, he came to me for a hug and asked me if Mrs. Foster is now in heaven with daddy.

I said yes, even though I hoped that was not the case. After what he did, I no longer believe Brett deserves to be in heaven.

This morning, Clark woke up excited to go to Mrs. Foster's funeral. I guess it was the idea of going out that brought on the excitement. I didn't blame him. Being indoors is driving us both crazy. I hate that he will only be able to say goodbye to Mrs. Foster from a distance. But it's the much safer option.

"Why can't we go to where the people are?" he asks when he notices that we're not getting out of the car. "I want to see Mrs. Foster."

I look at his face for a long time while searching for an answer. "Those people you see are Mrs. Foster's family. We were only her friends."

Like I used to do as a kid, I secretly cross the fingers of my left hand, the ones that are out of his view, hoping he won't throw a fit and insist on us going to the grave.

I'm relieved when he gets back to driving the train Tasha gave him across the back of the passenger's seat.

I turn my attention to the group of mourners in the distance, gathered under an oak, in a small cemetery full of beautiful flowers and trees, benches to sit on, and ponds scattered around.

Given that we're a few blocks from the cemetery, on the opposite side of the street, it's hard to make out any faces. In my mind, I can hear the sound of people weeping. I see the casket being lowered into the ground. I feel the wind blowing through the leaves on the oak tree. I feel it sweeping across my damp cheek. The smells of cut grass and damp earth drift through the window.

As hard as it is to believe Mrs. Foster is gone, I'm glad she's no longer in emotional pain. She will never experience disappointment again. Wherever Mrs. Foster is, I hope if she's able to see us down here, to see that even though we are not among the other mourners, we still showed up.

There's a soft tap on the passenger's window.

I turn and meet the eyes of the police officer, whose name I can't remember immediately due to the fog in my mind. I'd like to think he does not recognize me either, but he does know my car from the day he followed me home.

I should not have come. I should not have left the motel. I have made a lot of stupid mistakes in my life, but this is perhaps one of the worst. Willow Creek is too small of a town for me to stay anonymous here. They're still searching for me.

My lips are parted, but I can't speak. Being caught off guard like this makes it hard for me to think. I consider starting the car and driving off, but that would be even more stupid. He had followed me once before and he would probably do it again.

"Who is that policeman, Mommy?" Clark asks from the backseat. His voice is distant through the rush in my ears.

I do what a normal person would do, someone who has nothing to hide from the cops. I roll down the window and try to keep my breathing controlled.

"It's someone I know, baby," I say to Clark and turn back to the police officer.

He cannot see through the glasses I'm wearing, but my eyes are pleading with him not to do something that would scar my son for life.

Don't arrest me in front of my son, I beg without words.

"I thought that was you," he says, and a shiver of fear vibrates down my spine. "I remember the car."

Of course, he does. He's a police officer. They're trained to recognize these things. They pay attention to detail.

"Good afternoon, Officer." The dryness in my throat tickles out a cough.

He smiles. "I'm surprised to see you here. I've been going to Lemon from time to time, and I haven't seen you in a while."

I clench my hands into fists, digging my nails into my palms.

"Yes." I'm trying to be brave, to be normal so he doesn't get suspicious. "I don't work there anymore."

"I heard. That's a shame. Why did you stop?"

That's exactly why I never wanted to speak to him. He would ask questions. His job is to ask a lot of them, in different ways, so he can get to the truth.

I shrug. "I wanted something different, that's all. It was a temporary thing."

"Is that your son back there?" He peers through the window to the backseat.

I glance behind me, and notice that Clark has removed his cap. I need to keep talking, to distract him so he does not focus too much on Clark and get a chance to memorize his features.

"Yes, that's my son. How have you been doing?" Diverting the conversation to him might be the best option for me right now.

"I've been well, busy chasing criminals." He gives me a bright smile. Maybe he thinks I'm finally interested in him. That won't be good either. "Are you here for old Mrs. Foster's funeral?" He's saying her name as if he knew her personally, as if he didn't come to town only a couple of weeks ago.

"Yes, we are," I say.

"Then why are you not going to join the others?"

"It's...it's too hard. I—"

"I understand." His lips stretch into a warm smile. "Did you know her well?"

I shake my head on instinct. "Not that well, but enough."

"Yes, Mommy. We know Mrs. Foster. She was my fairy grandmother."

The officer laughs and peers at Clark through the window again. "Your fairy grandmother, huh? I heard she was a nice lady."

He's probably wishing I would roll down the window so he can get a good look at Clark.

"Yes," Clark presses his nose against the window, flattening it. "She's in heaven now."

"Well, yes, you're right. She is." He returns to the front window. "This might not be the right time, but would you mind if I ask you a few questions? It might be best if you step out." He glances into the backseat at Clark again.

It's never a good sign when a police officer

wants to question someone. And of course, I can't refuse, unless I have something to hide, which I don't want him to believe I do.

"Um, sure." I get out of the car.

Outside the car, I run my hands up and down my arms. When I remember that body language says a lot more than words, I drop my arms again. "What is it, Officer? What do you want to know?"

A river of sweat is already making its way down my back. What if this is it? What if this is where it ends?

He walks over to my side of the car, gravel crunching beneath his feet. "I don't mean to take you away from your son. Since you're here, I might as well ask you some routine questions we're asking anyone who knew Mrs. Foster. When was the last time you saw her?"

I lift my shoulders and allow them to drop again. "It's been a few days. I can't really remember."

"You no longer live in her cabin. Is there a reason why you moved out?"

How does he know that I moved out? Did he drop by? Does it even matter now?

"Like I said, sometimes things are temporary." My voice sounds harsher than I want it to be.

He waits for me to say more. When I don't,

he nods.

"So, you don't remember the last time you last saw Mrs. Foster?" He pulls out his notebook and starts jotting down my answers. All my lies are about to be recorded in black and white.

"No." I discreetly press my palms against the sides of my thighs so my jeans can soak up the sweat.

"Did you have an argument with Mrs. Foster? Is that why you left the cabin?"

"No," I repeat. "We never had an argument." Of course, I cannot tell the officer that she asked me to leave without getting myself into trouble.

"Is there anything more you want to know?" I ask. "I actually promised to take my son to the park." I still haven't removed my glasses and I'm glad he doesn't ask me to.

He puts away his notebook and smiles, shaking his head, but his face lingers on mine for a moment too long. "No, that's all." His intense gaze unnerves me. "I didn't want to keep you. There are just a few unanswered questions when it comes to Mrs. Foster's death."

My breath catches in my throat. "What do you mean?"

He taps his fingers against his lips, his eyes

still trained on my face. "It seems that her death was not from natural causes. The autopsy results have shown that she was poisoned."

CHAPTER 33

I collapse against the car, shock and despair twisting and turning inside me.

"Mrs. Foster was killed?" I ask, sorrow closing my throat. The news is too bitter for me to swallow.

"It's possible," Officer Roland says. I remember his name now. "I was hoping you know something that might help with the investigation."

"I don't..." My mouth opens. My mouth closes again.

Clark is pressing his entire face against the window now, his hands on both sides of his head as he blows warm air onto the glass to create a mist. I wonder if he could hear what we were just saying.

"I don't understand," I murmur.

From the corner of my eye, I catch movement, then sounds make their way to us, the voices of the people who came to Mrs.

Foster's funeral. The burial is over, and they are dispersing. Some of them might come in our direction.

I need to leave, but I can't do so without arousing Officer Roland's suspicions.

"Yeah, we also don't understand why anyone would want to kill a woman who everyone insists was a good person."

"Yes. She was… She was a wonderful person." I wish I could remove my glasses so my tears could flow freely. "I don't get it." I run a palm over my forehead. "I'm sorry. I… we have to go. I have to take Clark to—"

"Clark," the officer repeats the name and I give myself an inward kick. "Lovely name for a lovely boy." He continues to stare at me as though he's trying to figure me out.

More people are walking around us now and I'm becoming increasingly nervous. I wish he would stop talking to me and let me go. The longer I stand outside, the more likely it will be that someone else will recognize me.

"Officer," I say, "There are several people here who might know what happened. You might want to question them before they leave."

"You might be right. I guess I should get on with it. Thank you for your time, Zoe."

I'm about to get into my car when I catch

sight of Tasha emerging from the crowds. Too late, she sees me. She stops walking and her husband, who's next to her, continues to walk on, holding the hands of their two boys.

My eyes lock with Tasha's, and her lips curl into a warm smile.

"I'll see you around," Officer Roland says. "By the way, where are you staying at the moment?"

I want to tell him that I'm not planning to stick around, but then he would insist that I *should* stay. I don't want him to get any more suspicious, so I tell him.

I give him the name of the motel, knowing well that the only thing we'll do when we get back there is to get our things and move to another place. The number I give him is that of my second sim card, the one I used to call the police in Fort Haven, instead of the one I keep in my phone.

"Thank you, Zoe. Talk to you soon."

It makes me nervous that he still knows my name and now also Clark's.

Tasha is making her way toward me now, a faint smile still on her lips.

"Zoe," she says when she gets close enough for me to hear her. Her eyes look swollen from crying, and she's wearing a black cocktail dress, her hair in two braids flat on her scalp.

She wraps me in a hug. Taken aback, I don't hug her back immediately. My arms remain limp at my sides until the desire to connect with someone else brings me to put my arms around her as well.

I don't know how long we stand there, holding each other, saying so much without words. My glasses are no longer able to prevent my tears from sliding down my cheeks.

Finally, we let go, but Tasha keeps her hands on my shoulders. "Are you okay?"

I nod and dig inside my jeans pocket to pull out a tissue. "I am. I'm okay." That's what everyone says even when they're far from being fine.

"I didn't think you would come."

"I didn't think I would come either."

I remove my glasses and wipe my eyes with a crumpled tissue.

"It's good that you came. The way Mrs. Foster spoke about you, it was clear you meant a lot to her." Tasha glances in the direction of her husband and kids. "You should join us for the wake we're hosting."

"Thanks, but I don't think it's a good idea." I want to accept her invitation, but I can't. I'm pretty sure Officer Roland will be around, questioning everyone. He might think of more questions to ask me.

"I'm sorry to hear that." Tasha pauses. "If it makes you feel any better, Ronan is not here. He's still behind bars. Apparently, when he was informed of his mother's death, he said he didn't care."

"That's terrible." How can he be so cold, especially after everything he put her through?

"I know." Tasha shakes her head ruefully, then looks me up and down. "You've lost a lot of weight. Are you sure you're okay? You don't look well."

"I'm tired." It's an honest answer. I'm tired of running, tired of hiding, tired of hurting. I want to be able to lie in bed and not worry about tomorrow. It feels like I haven't slept for a year, and when I do sleep, the nightmares come to find me.

"I'm sorry, Tasha. I actually have to go. I need to take Clark somewhere." I reach for the door handle.

"Did you hear that Mrs. Foster was poisoned?" she says before I get back into the car.

"Yes," I whisper. "The police officer just told me. I don't know who would want to hurt her."

"Me neither. If Ronan were not in prison, I would have suspected him immediately."

Worry snakes through me. If it wasn't

Ronan, and the Willow Creek residents loved Mrs. Foster, maybe it was someone from out of town.

Overcome with the need to flee again, I yank open the door and get inside. "I... I should go... I'm sorry."

I leave her standing on the sidewalk, a confused expression on her face.

As soon as we get to the motel, I pack our things and we're back in the car. The only stop we make on our way out of town is to get some groceries. We will be spending another few days indoors.

I don't want to think I could be right. I'm wrestling to keep my thoughts from going to a terrifying place, but that's exactly where I end up.

If Ronan did not kill his mother, what if Cole killed her because she offered me shelter? What if Mrs. Foster died because of me? If we had never come into her life, would she still be alive?

Fear like I've never known before is coursing through my veins as I drive as far away from Willow Creek as I can.

But does it really matter where I go and how fast I run? If Cole had found out that I was in Willow Creek, what would stop him from finding me anywhere else?

I would like to think that Cole would be too busy trying to hide from the cops instead of chasing after me, but the truth remains that Mrs. Foster died the day they said he disappeared. As long as he's out there, there's no telling what he is capable of, which means we are in danger.

Maybe he knows I'm behind his downfall and he's now more determined than ever to get revenge, destroying anything or anyone in his path to me.

We drive for an hour until we reach Maple Lane, a town an hour south of Willow Creek. I'm too exhausted both physically and emotionally to drive any further, so I stop at an isolated roadside motel.

A bored-looking man chewing gum with his mouth open checks us in. Behind him, there are only two other empty spaces on the rack. It seems only two other rooms are occupied in the entire place. No wonder he looks bored.

In front of the door to our room is a folded newspaper. I pick it up and as soon as I unfold it, Cole's face stares back at me. Fear paralyzes me as I stare into his cold, murderous eyes. They look alive even on a page, like they're mocking me, warning me that he's near and will soon catch up with me.

Does the fact that the newspaper is at my

door mean that he's at this motel? Surely, he wouldn't have known that this is the room I would be given. And yet, the newspaper looks like some kind of warning.

I'm about to grab Clark and escape to another motel, but I relax when I notice that the same rolled-up newspaper is on the doorsteps of the other doors as well. Mine wasn't targeted. I fold up the newspaper and shove it into my bag.

Inside the room, the walls are so thin that we can hear music being played in the room next door. I find it soothing until I recognize it and my stomach starts to churn.

Let's freeze our memories, baby.

It's my wedding song, the song we played on every anniversary except the last one.

Pain erupts inside my belly. My wedding song will never have the same effect on me again.

In Brett's arms the night of our wedding, I thought everything would be ok, that we would make it through anything, that I would heal. How wrong I was. How stupid I was.

CHAPTER 34

I stand in the doorway of the bathroom, my gaze sweeping the entire room from wall to wall.

I can't see him. I can't see Clark. I left him in the room and now he's gone.

The cold knot of fear clenches inside my belly.

"Clark," I call out, searching the small room as though it were some huge living space with lots of places for a little boy to hide. I drop to my knees and search underneath the bed. Maybe he's playing hide and seek with me.

He's not. I can't see or hear him move. The only thing under the bed is dead, dusty air.

He's nowhere to be seen.

For a heartbeat, everything around me stops. It feels as if my heart has also stopped beating.

No. This can't be happening. I have to be dreaming.

When it hits me that this is not a dream, life comes back to my limbs, and I dive for the door. My pulse pounds in the side of my neck, and my throat closes more tightly with each passing second that I don't see my son.

I had only been in the bathroom for a few minutes. I was desperate for time alone, time away to weep without Clark seeing me.

Normally, whenever I was not in the room with him, I secured the door with the chain lock, but it's now dangling free. What if I had forgotten to do it and Clark climbed on something to reach it?

I never got the idea that he would think of going out on his own. I shouldn't have left him alone. How could I have been so reckless?

He's been bugging me for two days to go outside. He wanted to go to the park. The answer was always 'no' and that, of course, frustrated him. He responded with escalating tantrums that were starting to wear both of us out.

He had reached his breaking point and so had I, but we had no choice, we had to stay hidden at least for a few days. I was waiting to hear that Cole is back in police custody.

I yank open the door and burst outside. I don't care that I'm in my pajamas and bare feet. My son is missing and all I care about is finding him.

"Where are you, Clark?" My voice is shrill as I yell for my son.

I can't waste time. I need to find him before he gets far. Every second feels like an hour.

A pall of dread hangs over me as I frantically search the grounds around the motel.

What if Cole took him? What if Clark did not walk out on his own, and instead Cole showed up while I was crying in the bathroom and took him away?

Left with no other choice but to ask for help, I bolt to the reception area. The same man who had given us the keys when we arrived is still there, still bored.

The place smells of burnt coffee and sweat.

He looks up from his newspaper and gives a low grunt. "What do you want?" he asks, as if I'm being a nuisance even though I'm a guest.

"My son is missing."

He drags a hand through his greasy hair. "And what does that have to do with me? I'm not his babysitter."

"Yes, yes, I know." I was the one who was supposed to look out for Clark, and my guilt is heavy in my chest. If I don't find him, I'll never forgive myself. "Please help me find him."

"Sorry, I can't help you there." He looks back to his paper. "I'm busy."

"You're reading a newspaper." The bite in my tone takes both of us by surprise.

"Lady, your son is not my responsibility. He's probably hiding. Kids do silly things like that. That's why I never wanted any."

He's right. It's not his fault that Clark is missing. "Please help me," I beg. "I searched everywhere."

He lowers his newspaper again and raises his eyebrow. "Everywhere?"

He has a point. I haven't searched everywhere—just around the motel and the parking lot. There's still a large part of town I have not explored. Surely, Clark wouldn't be too far from the motel. I had been in the bathroom for no longer than a few minutes. There's no way he can be far.

Determined to find him, I run back to my room and grab my car keys. I drive around the area. This time of evening, there are only a handful of people on the street and none of them is my son.

I should never have left his side. I thought he would be occupied with his toys for a while. Until now, I have resisted the urge to cry because it would make things too real. Now I can't hold back. The tears come, flowing hard and hot down my cheeks.

I'm tempted to go all the way into the center

of town, but I'm still afraid to get too far in case Clark is wandering near the motel. Maybe he just went out for a walk and couldn't find his way back. It feels like I'm stuck in a nightmare.

If someone finds him, they might alert the cops, which would be both a relief and a nightmare, because if they find out who I am, I might never get Clark back. Who would give a child to someone who is considered to be a murderer?

Every boy I see during my drive looks like my son, but Clark is nowhere to be seen. The people I ask haven't seen a little boy walking around on his own. They simply shake their heads and continue on with their lives while mine is at a standstill.

I drive around in circles for a while, then I drive back to the motel to check if he has somehow shown up. I left the door open just in case.

Apart from a taxi parked in the lot, with no driver inside, nothing has changed in the area and Clark is still not in our room. I go around knocking on doors.

The only people who open their door is a thirty-something-year-old Asian woman and a teenage girl who looks like she could be her daughter.

They don't have the good news I'm

desperate for. They haven't seen him, and I'm starting to worry that he didn't actually go off on his own, but someone took him.

"Are you sure he's not in your room?" the woman asks when I start crying again.

"No, he's not." I bury my hands in my hair. "I can't find him."

"Has he done something like this before? I mean...run off on his own?"

"No." I shake my head. "Never."

"Then you have to call the police," the woman says. "They will find him."

"I don't know," I say. Can I really call the cops? For months, I have been doing everything to stay away from them. Now I might have to go to them because I have no other choice. If I don't ask them for help and something happens to Clark, I would never forgive myself.

The woman and her daughter are kind enough to help me look around the perimeter of the motel again with no success. They apologize for not being able to help me and return to their room.

The sun is starting to set and Clark is still out there.

The woman was right, I need to get the police involved. If I end up going to prison, so be it. At least I won't have to worry about them giving him to Cole since he will eventually end up in prison as well.

I return to my room to get my phone, but it's not on the bedside table where I left it before I went searching for Clark.

My body stiffens in horror at the realization that someone might have been inside the room.

Cole.

I may not be able to see him, but I would recognize his expensive cologne anywhere. Mixed with the faint scent of cigars, it's lingering in the air, taunting my nostrils.

The toxins of hate and terror blaze through my veins as I run back to reception to ask if I can use the phone. Now that I'm certain Cole is involved, I will call the cops for sure.

The bored man is no longer behind the reception desk.

I'm about to leave when he walks in from outside, eating a burger. Ketchup is dripping onto his chin and clinging to his beard.

"You again," he says, chewing. When he raises the burger to his mouth again, I notice his expensive Rolex glinting in the light.

"I need to call the police. Please, can I use your phone? I can't find mine."

He shakes his head. "It's not working."

He's lying. He doesn't want to help me and

I don't understand why. A child is missing and he doesn't seem to care at all.

"I'm begging you. My son is still missing. I need to call the police. Someone took him."

"Ma'am, as I said, my phone is not working." He pushes the nail of his pinkie between his two front teeth to remove whatever is stuck there. He continues to eat his burger as he disappears through a door behind the reception desk.

I scan the surface for the phone, but I can't see it. Maybe he was telling the truth.

I charge back outside. I will ask the Asian woman and her daughter. They will help me.

My skin is hot, my hands clammy, my feet feeling too heavy. The faster I walk, the more I feel like I'm slowing down.

To my disappointment, I spot a car pulling out of the parking lot. It's the people I wanted to ask for help. I run after the car, but it has already turned into the main road.

The room next to ours has the light on. I go slam my fists against it. Sweat is pouring into my eyes, mixing with my tears.

"Come in," a man calls from the other side. Relieved, I push down the door handle.

When the door swings open, I reel back in shock.

"Mommy." Clark looks up and our eyes

meet. "Look, grandpa came to visit us."

I wish it weren't true, but it is. Clark is on the couch, sitting next to my worst nightmare.

"Surprised to see me?" Cole raises an eyebrow, his face twisting into a grin.

CHAPTER 35

He's sitting there with a saintly expression, like someone who isn't rotting with evil. He's even wearing one of his designer suits. You'd think he's about to attend a meeting, not on the run from the law.

"Let him go." I choke out the words, and my body shakes so much my teeth are chattering. I have never been more terrified of anyone in my life or so overcome with the kind of hate that rips you apart and does nothing to hurt its object.

My gut had told me that he was responsible for Clark's disappearance, but I was hoping it was wrong.

He tightens his arms around Clark and sneers at me.

My eyes grow hot with rage, especially when I take in the pale watch-shaped mark circling his wrist. It all makes sense. The reason the motel receptionist wouldn't help me was because Cole got to him first. He paid him with his own Rolex.

"After all this time, no hello?" he asks. "I'm quite disappointed, Meghan. Or is it Zoe now?"

"Let go of my son." I ball my hands into fists. "Clark, baby, come to Mommy." I unfurl my fingers and stretch out my arms for him to run into.

Clark shakes his head and leans into Cole. "I want to stay with grandpa. We had fun. Grandpa bought me ice cream. We left you some in the fridge, Mommy."

I notice two things at once, that there really is a mini fridge in this room, and that Clark is playing with an expensive-looking black and gold toy plane.

My mind fills in the blanks. All the hours I spent wondering how far Cole had gotten, he was right next door to us with only a wall between.

He's the person who played my wedding song next door when we first arrived. He probably heard the shower running when I turned it on to drown out my sobs and came to lure Clark away with the toy. He must have seen him sitting alone through the sheer curtains.

Of course, Clark opened the door. Cole is

not a stranger, but someone he trusts, his family. Those we trust are often the most dangerous.

Even if the chain lock were secure in place, it would have been easy for Cole to slip his hand through the crack in the door to lift the chain out of its metal casing. Or maybe the motel receptionist helped him.

Cole raises one of his hands and runs it over my son's hair. "I missed you, my boy," he says to Clark.

"Cole, please, don't do this." I'm seething with rage, but I have to control my temper for Clark's sake.

His gaze still on me, he gets to his feet and reaches into his pocket for a phone, my phone. He hands it to Clark. "Go and play a game in the bathroom. Your Mommy and I need to speak about something important." He ruffles his hair. "Go on, boy. Don't come out until I tell you to, then soon I'll let you fly on a real airplane."

The bathroom is the only other room in the motel rooms, the only opportunity to escape from the bedroom.

"Really? Yay!" Clark's eyes light up as he beams up at Cole. Then he does as he's told.

As soon as the door closes, I rush to it and plant myself in front. I'm trying to protect

Clark, but I don't know if I'll succeed. "What do you want from me?" I whisper furiously. "Why don't you leave us alone?"

Cole strokes his stubble. "You know exactly what I want from you, black widow."

"I didn't." I lower my voice. "I didn't kill my husband and you know it. We both know you did, and you tried to frame me."

Cole guffaws, then lowers himself into the couch again. He's so relaxed, as if he's in no hurry at all, not like someone who's wanted by the cops.

"That's the story you've been telling yourself all these months?"

"It's the truth. You're evil. You're not only a murderer. You... all those things... I know what you did to all those women, you disgusting pig. You did to them what you did to me."

"Oh, I remember that night." He narrows his eyes. "Why didn't you tell Brett the truth, that I owned you before he did?"

I clench my fists. I want to lunge for him, to claw out his eyes, to leave my mark of revenge. He knows very well why I didn't. He knows I wanted to. Torturing me is his favorite game.

"Please, Cole. Leave us in peace. I won't... I won't tell anyone you were here."

"You think it's that simple?" He shakes his

head, plants his hands on his thighs and pushes to his full height. "I've been waiting for this moment for so long. You know what? For a while there, I thought of letting you be, allowing you to spend the rest of your pathetic life looking over your shoulder. But I changed my mind. Life's too short not to have a little fun, wouldn't you say? I needed to find you, to finish what I started. I wanted to destroy you." He shoves his hands into his pockets. "Plus, you took Liam away from me."

I press my back against the bathroom door. "You'll never do to him what you did to Brett." I inhale sharply. "I won't let you."

"I won't allow you to keep him from me, Meghan. Wherever you go, I'll be right behind you. I'll be forever your shadow." He chuckles. "It was quite entertaining getting calls from so many people who claimed to have seen you. They all wanted the $20,000. As I had expected, most of them ignored the cops and came straight to me asking for a higher reward. Many were liars, except one honest man, who told me about the old woman who was letting you stay in her cabin."

Sheer terror sweeps through me.

"You did it." I choke back a cry. "You...you…"

"I've done a lot of things, Meghan. Which

one are you talking about?"

"You killed her. You killed Mrs. Foster."

"That was her name? I had no idea."

He's not admitting to the crime, but he may as well have. It's written all over his face. His murderous smile tells me everything I need to know. He has committed so many evil deeds that I don't know which of them is the worst.

"How could you?" My voice is low and tortured. "How could you kill an innocent woman?"

"It wasn't me who killed her. It was you, Meghan. You came into her life. If you had stayed away, if she had not helped you, she would probably still be alive. But then again, she was a weak and frail old woman. She was going to die anyway."

"No." I try to keep standing, but my legs give way. I can't stop myself from sinking to the floor.

He's right. I knew from the start that allowing Mrs. Foster to help me was putting her in danger. But I was desperate.

"The worst thing is that you cut me out of the boy's life and allowed a stranger to look after him."

My mouth opens, then closes. My throat is too tight to let any words out.

"I knew everything, Meghan. I had someone

keeping an eye on you." His mouth twists into a grin. "Don't look so surprised. I warned you that I would find you."

"Who?" The word comes out like a bullet. It has to be Ronan who tipped him off. I knew from the start that he would be my downfall.

Cole runs a hand through his thick hair. "That cop you've been seeing around, he's one of my men." He rubs his hands together. "We actually didn't know each other until he called for his reward. It's always a good idea to have several cops on one's side, and usually a lot of money does the trick. I offered him more if he kept an eye on you for me and carried out other chores, like leaving that squirrel at your doorstep. Watching you scrub away the blood was incredibly satisfying."

I gape at him, speechless. Roland is a crooked cop? And here I was thinking he was interested in me. No wonder I felt so uncomfortable around him. I thought it had to do with the simple reason that he was a cop.

"I don't blame him for coming to me. He had gambling debts and child support to pay, and he wasn't paid enough for his service."

"What do you want from me?" I croak.

Behind me, on the other side, a tiny voice makes itself known through the thin door. "Can I come out now?" Clark calls.

"Not yet, my boy." Cole smiles at me. "Very soon."

"Okay," Clark squeals with delight. "Then we can go flying?"

"Yes, then we'll go on a fun adventure. We'll also go fishing and I'll teach you to hunt at my cabin."

His words make me want to throw up. Once a month, he and Brett went hunting at his cabin in a small village near Fort Lake. Brett hated going, but he never said no. When Clark was two, he took us with him. When Cole saw that Brett had brought the two of us along, he exploded with anger and left. We ended up spending the weekend at the cabin, just the three of us. We fished, we went for walks in the small town, and bought fresh fruits and vegetables from the locals.

Cole takes a step forward, his face darker. "You messed with my business. You called people and told them damaging things about me."

How did he find out? How did he know that I was behind it all? Could he have been stalking Denise's mother?

"You deserve to go to prison for what you did." I lower my voice. "You are a murderer and a rapist."

"And you made a big mistake. You should

have stayed out of my business. Those women, most of them were prostitutes. They offered themselves willingly to me and to everyone else who visited the hotel."

The same words Marjorie had used when defending him.

"I wasn't… Denise wasn't a prostitute. You raped her. You killed her." I inhale sharply. "You killed Janella."

"There are exceptions to every rule," he sighs and shoves his hands into his pockets. "Denise was too much trouble and Janella, well, you can try and figure it out yourself." He turns to the window, his back to me.

The image of Janella's phone lying on the kitchen counter that night comes to me. She probably came back for it and saw Cole killing Brett. Then she ran. My heart jumps to my throat. "She saw you kill Brett."

"Maybe, maybe not." He lifts the curtain to look out into the darkness.

That has to be it. That's why she wanted to speak to me moments before Clark and I left the house. She wanted to tell me what she saw. Maybe she planned to go to the cops, but she was afraid of Cole. I'll always regret not hearing her out that morning.

I need to take my son and get away from Cole before I become his next victim.

Physically, Clark is safe from him. He wouldn't kill his own grandson, a child. But then, Cole has shown himself to be capable of more than I could ever imagine.

Adrenaline floods back into my body and I slowly rise to my feet.

While his back is still turned to me, I twist the bathroom handle and pull open the door. Thankfully, Clark is right behind it. I grab his arm and pull him out.

"Ouch, Mommy," he complains, and Cole turns back to face me, thunderclouds in his eyes.

"What do you think you're doing? Don't make another stupid mistake."

Ignoring him, I push Clark toward the front door, standing between him and Cole. "Go to the car, Clark. It's open."

"But, mom, grandpa…"

"I said go. Now. Run." My voice is firmer than he has ever heard it, so he opens the door and runs out, still holding my phone.

When Cole takes a step toward me, I grab a standing lamp from nearby and raise it above my head. "Don't you dare come near me or my son."

I wait until the car door slams.

"You never learn, do you?" Cole drawls. "You can't win this game. I'm the cat and you're the mouse. Go ahead and walk out that door. See how far you'll get." He comes even closer.

I don't waste time. I swing the lamp as hard as I can. It collides with his body, and he loses his balance and topples into the TV, sending it crashing to the floor, with him following right after it.

I'm about to run out of the room when he starts laughing. He's still on the floor, but even in a weakened position, he has a hold on me.

"I know you planned to kill Brett," he says. "I also knew you were too weak to get the job done."

"So, you stepped in to finish the job?" There's no point in denying anything. Brett probably told Cole that he asked me to help him die.

"Yes, I was involved in his death. Brett deserved to go. He was a coward."

I need to go to the cops, but not the ones in this town. He probably already got to some of them. There are good cops in other towns. Not all of them are crooked. At least I hope they aren't.

"Go to hell." I grab the door again and step out.

"I won't let you take my son from me," he shouts. His words slam against my heart, and I almost stumble with shock, but I keep moving until I'm behind the wheel.

The moment I start the car, he appears in the doorway and runs to the taxi I saw sitting in the parking lot earlier.

CHAPTER 36

It can't be true.

Cole is not Clark's father. I never had a DNA test done because a few days after the rape, I had my period. How much more confirmation could I need?

He lied. He knew I was slipping out of his grasp, so he threw a blow where he knew it would hurt the most.

"You're driving too fast, Mommy," Clark says for the fourth time.

I peer into the rearview mirror and tension melts from my shoulders.

Not a single car is behind us. We lost him.

Cole's taxi was behind us for at least half an hour, not speeding, just torturing me. It's what he does best.

"I'm sorry, baby." I take a quick glance at Clark and I shudder inwardly.

He *does* resemble Cole. I'd never noticed how much. He has the same squinting, slate-gray eyes and slightly upturned nose.

What if?

It's not possible.

Clark is Brett's son, not Cole's. It's no surprise that he resembles Cole. Even if I wish they weren't related, they are.

The cramps of fear in my belly refuse to give me relief, and the little voice inside my head continues to ask, 'what if?'

Something inside me is unfurling to life, forcing its way to the surface, a possibility that refuses to be stifled.

The day I gave birth to Clark, I did wonder if I should do a DNA test to be sure. My online research at the time had revealed that on rare occasions, there are women who claimed to have had their periods while pregnant.

For weeks I was tempted to do the test, but I eventually scrapped the thought. If it turned out that Clark was Cole's son, it would have eaten me alive and destroyed my marriage. I would have been forced to tell Brett what his father did to me. He would never have recovered from that betrayal. I would have lost him, and Cole would have won the war against our relationship.

"Mommy, why are you angry with grandpa?" The question makes me feel like someone has shoved me into a brick wall.

What do I tell Clark? I can't possibly allow him to continue thinking Cole is a saint. I have worked so hard to protect him from the truth. But right now, I can't find the strength. Seeing Cole and almost losing Clark have drained me.

"I'm sorry, baby, but your grandfather is not a good person. Promise me that you will not go anywhere with him again. He did some bad things."

"What did he do? Did he hurt you?"

You have no idea. You have no idea how much he hurt me. What he did to me I cannot put into words.

That's what I want to tell him, but I can't. That part of the truth he cannot know, at least not yet. I don't want to shatter his innocence completely. But eventually, I might not have a choice. Cole's crimes have become a national story. Clark is bound to see him on the news, or some random person might even tell him.

"He wants to hurt us." It's the truth. Even if Cole might not want to hurt Clark physically, he could destroy him emotionally, as he did to Brett. Cole would mold him into the person he wants him to be, his puppet, his weapon. He would also use him as a tool to make himself feel powerful. He would pulverize my son's confidence in order to build his own.

"But he's nice," Clark says. "I miss him."

"No, he's not, Clark. He's not a nice person," I say between clenched teeth. "I need you to understand that. I need you to trust Mommy right now. And we need to get away from him."

"Is that why he didn't visit us in the cabin?"

"Yes." I tighten my hands around the steering wheel, speeding up. "We can't let him come near us again."

A car has appeared behind us, its headlights blinking on and off. A warning?

My fear starts pushing me to the edge of my sanity again, but then the car turns into another road. I wipe my forehead with the back of my hand and release the breath I'd been holding.

How long until he shows up again? What if he's ahead of us, waiting in the darkness? But he doesn't know where we are headed. Neither do I. My plan so far has been to get as far away from him as possible, but I have no destination in mind.

It's only a few minutes later that I notice we are actually twenty minutes from Willow Creek. It feels like I'm going home. I did feel safe there for a while. That's where I have a friend.

I definitely need one at this moment. I'm too tired to continue doing it alone.

I'm scared that Cole might hurt Tasha if she

helps me, but I need her. I need to at least speak to her. She did promise that she will be there for me. It's time to cash in the promise.

I pick up the phone and pull in a breath, then I dial. When she picks up, I'm unable to say the words on my mind because my throat is closing up with emotion.

"Zoe," she says. "Honey, is that you?"

"I need your help, Tasha," I blurt out. "Please, I don't know what to do. I don't know where to go."

I should probably go to the police, but what if Cole suspects that's what I will do and waits for me there? I have no idea how many more police officers he has corrupted. Maybe the reason he hasn't been found is that he has a team of police officers on his payroll.

I shudder when I think of Roland, the police officer, how he stalked me without my knowledge. He was watching me from the bushes all along.

My head hurts too much to think about what to do next. I need someone else to think for me, to tell me what to do.

"Where are you?" Tasha asks, her voice high-pitched with worry. "Are you okay?"

"No." My voice is smothered by tears. "I'm actually not okay. I'm in danger."

"Come to our house. Wherever you are,

come here, okay?"

"I can't." I want to. I want to find a safe place to hide, but if Cole is after me, I would lead him straight to the people who are trying to help me. I don't want anyone else to die because of me. "He's after me. If I come to you, you will be in danger, too."

I feel foolish. What was the point of calling Tasha if I'm refusing her help?

I guess calling her was to ensure that I'm not all alone in this.

But any minute now, I'll run out of gas and we'll be stranded.

"Who is after you?" she asks.

"My...my father-in-law. He's dangerous." I glance at Clark. He's on the verge of falling asleep. "I can't say more now."

Tasha is quiet. Perhaps she's wondering whether I'm really worth all the trouble or if she should give up.

"Tell me where you are. I'll come to you. Then you can tell me everything."

"I'm headed to Willow Creek," I say.

"Perfect. Let's meet at a crowded place somewhere."

"Where?" I don't know what place in Willow Creek would be crowded late at night.

"Come to my brother's club, The Night Owl. Ask for Samuel. I'll meet you there. How far away are you?"

"We should arrive in about fifteen or so minutes."

"I'm on my way."

Tasha's right. It would be best to meet in a crowded place. Cole would think twice before showing up there, especially since he's all over the news.

As for me, I may be wanted by the cops, but I look different now. However, it will be strange for me to walk into a club with a small child, but if that's the only place we will be safe, we have to do it.

I need to trust Tasha because I can't trust myself at the moment, not after I almost lost my son. After being careful for so long, I'm now making too many mistakes that could lead to me ending up in prison or worse.

If Cole ever finds me again, there's no doubt in my mind that he will kill me. I know too much about what he did. At the end of all of this, only one of us will be left standing.

CHAPTER 37

◦∽◦

People are spilling in and out of The Night Owl. It makes me feel even more confident that it's the perfect place to meet with Tasha.

I slow down first, observing the place, making sure that Cole is not among the people gathered outside the entrance. But then, if he were, he would be smart enough to camouflage himself, of course.

I ease my anxiety with the thought that he won't be able to do anything to me without someone stepping up or calling the cops. He will not risk being identified.

Instead of parking close to the club, I find a spot a few blocks away, close to a hotel. There's a chance that Cole will think I'm inside the hotel instead of the night club.

It was best for me not to go to the cops, where I could risk coming into contact with Roland.

When Clark opens his eyes, he's disoriented

for a moment. I feel terrible for waking him.

"Where are we?" he asks, looking out the window.

"We're going to see Tasha. Would you like that? We miss her, don't we?"

His face brightens up, but he only nods with a smile. Exhaustion is written all over his face. I dream of a day when we are settled, and he can rest without interruption.

"Sweetheart, listen to Mommy very carefully." I reach for his hand. "I need you to be a good boy, okay? If you see grandpa, don't go to him. Remember what I said to you?"

He nods. "He's not a nice man. He wants to hurt us."

I can tell he wants to ask more questions but doesn't know the right ones or how to phrase them.

"Are we going to Lemon?" he asks.

"No, we're not." I help him out of his car seat. "Tasha wants us to meet at another place."

"What will grandpa do if he finds us?"

"He won't," I say with determination.

Clark doesn't ask any more questions. In silence, I pull his baseball cap over his head and put mine on as well. Then we hurry hand in hand down the street. I glance over my shoulder every few seconds and peer into the windows of every car that passes.

Just because I don't see him doesn't mean he's not near.

We make it to the club without anything suspicious happening. The clubbers milling around the entrance glance at me with suspicion as they puff their cigarettes.

It's obvious they're judging me. What kind of mother would bring a child to a club when he should be in bed fast asleep?

The bouncer is a boulder of a man with half his head shaved and the other adorned by spiky hair. He's wearing a tight T-shirt, with the word 'Bouncer' across the front.

The way he's towering over me reminds me of Cole. They're both intimidating, but in different ways.

"Invitation only tonight." He throws Clark a look. "And no kids allowed."

I pull Clark closer to me. His little body is trembling as he buries his face into my side.

"We were invited to come here," I say.

Mr. Bouncer folds his arms across his chest. "Your name?"

"Zoe... Zoe is my name." Now that the past has caught up with me, saying my name is Zoe makes my stomach queasy. After this is all over, I'm not sure whether I will go back to my old name or keep this one. "Samuel is my friend's brother. She told us to come here."

The bouncer's face relaxes, and he places a hand on top of Clark's head. "I was just making sure. Samuel is expecting you. Go up to the bar." He steps aside and we make our way through the throng of people.

Clark is holding my hand with one hand and covering his ear with the other. The rock music is so loud, I feel my body vibrate. I can't even imagine how it must be for him.

The bartender leans across the counter, his arms folded on the surface. "What can I get you?" he shouts over the noise.

"We were told to come here. Samuel is expecting us."

"I'll get him." He looks down at Clark, who has just hopped up onto a high stool. "Sorry, he needs to get down from there. It's the law." The man disappears, and a woman with a straight ponytail immediately replaces him behind the bar as Clark hops back down again.

She fills a glass with orange juice and a straw and hands it to me. "For the little guy," she nods toward Clark. "On the house." She winks at me and I thank her.

Clark drinks the juice gratefully. He must be hungry as well. I'll have to find a way to get him something to eat.

Looking around me, I'm glad that most of

the guests are dressed appropriately and I won't have to worry about shielding Clark.

Only a few people are dancing. The rest are at the bar or sitting on red leather couches on one side of the dance floor.

Samuel, a man with short dreadlocks and dressed in a suit, finally comes to meet us, and like Tasha, he seems to be very friendly.

"I'm sorry you had to wait so long." He shakes my hand. "Come with me. Let's get the boy out of this loud place."

As we follow him down a carpeted corridor, I'm glad he's not wasting time by asking questions.

"Where are we going?" I ask, suddenly uneasy. I know Tasha, but her brother is still a stranger to me.

"I was told to keep you safe. That's what I'm doing." He leads us down a flight of stairs to a wine cellar.

As soon as the heavy door at the top of the stairs shuts, the noise dies. It's so quiet in the basement that I can hear my own heart thudding.

"Tasha said you needed a safe place. This is it. Make yourselves at home. She said she'd be here in about ten minutes."

It's a large wine cellar that also serves as an office. A wooden desk is piled high with papers and folders. The entire room smells of thick sandalwood and bergamot cologne.

Samuel doesn't ask me any questions. Instead he calls for someone to bring us more drinks and a cheeseburger for Clark.

We sit down on battered leather chairs opposite the dusty wine racks. "Thank you." I'm moved by the help I'm getting from a stranger.

"That's all right. Tasha mentioned you're in danger."

"Um...yeah. We—"

"You don't have to explain. All I'm going to say is that you picked the right person to help you out. She said you're a good friend of hers."

Warmth spreads through my chest. "Yes, yes, I am."

"Then anyone who is Tasha's friend is my friend. So, whatever help you need, I'm here. I'm going upstairs for a while to see if she's arrived. You stay here and don't come up under any circumstances. The key is in the lock. Lock the door if it makes you feel safer."

As soon as he leaves, that's exactly what I do. Then I sit down and watch Clark eating his burger like he hasn't eaten in days.

Only about five minutes after Samuel leaves, someone knocks on the door. I'm afraid to open it, afraid it might be Cole, but Tasha calls my name from the other side.

The first thing she does when I open the door is gather me into her arms.

"Thank God you're okay." She pulls me closer.

I hold on to her as if for dear life. "Thank you so much for everything, Tasha."

I only hope she won't regret helping me after she discovers who I really am, and who I'm running from.

From over her shoulder, Samuel gives me a nod and merges with his guests, leaving us alone to talk.

It's time for the truth to come out. If Tasha is going to help me, I need to be honest with her about everything.

I start from the very beginning. I tell her how Cole raped me, how I married his son, how Brett was diagnosed with cancer and begged me to end his life, and everything that happened after.

"Please tell me you really didn't kill your husband," she says after a long silence, moving closer so Clark wouldn't hear our conversation. He's wearing headphones and watching cartoons on Tasha's phone while lying on a couch in a corner.

I shake my head. "No, I didn't, I swear. I almost...but I couldn't." I shut my eyes. "He died anyway. I thought he killed himself, but not anymore. His father did it. I know he did."

"Oh, my God." She covers her mouth in shock. "The maid as well?" Tasha was already familiar with the story from the news, so I don't have to fill in all the details. "You think he did that too?"

I nod.

She takes hold of my hands. "I already knew who you were. Mrs. Foster told me not long before she died."

"And you still want to help me?"

"I do because I don't believe you did it. I haven't known you for long, but my gut tells me you're not a murderer."

"I'm so scared, Tasha, for me and Clark. If he finds us again, he'll kill me and take my son. I can't let him. When he showed up at the motel and took Clark, I almost died." The fear I had felt at finding Clark gone returns to cut off my air supply.

"Then we won't let that monster come near him again. Clark is your son and you have the right to protect him. I'll do whatever I can to help you, but I think you should go to the police. Tell them everything. They might believe you. I believe you."

"But Cole has connections. That police officer that you thought was interested in me, he worked for him. He's the one who told him where I was. Cole has a lot of money to pay crooked cops. I don't know if I can trust any of them."

Tasha's mouth falls open. "You're kidding."

"No. Cole is the one who told me about the cop. I guess he was a decent policeman until he saw the reward on my head and called Cole."

"It makes sense now. The man has not been seen since the day he showed up at Mrs. Foster's funeral. He used to come to the restaurant almost every day, then he stopped. Who knows? Maybe he was fired or he left to spend his dirty money elsewhere."

"He's gone? Thank God." Now that I know the truth about him, I was terrified that he might still be stalking me.

"Yes, but your father-in-law could be anywhere. He needs to go to prison for his crimes, and you need to stop running." She pulls me into another hug and squeezes me tight. "I wish you had told me sooner. You didn't have to go through all that alone."

"Tasha," I push away, "there's something else you should know. It was Cole who killed Mrs. Foster. He admitted it."

Tasha's eyes flood with tears. "He...he did it? Why?"

"It was because she helped me." I pause. "If

you help me, you'll be in danger too."

"You don't have to worry about me. You need to take that evidence to the cops. You will only be free and safe if he's behind bars." She puts her hands on my shoulders. "I know it's terrifying, but that man can't get away with murder and rape. You have the power to make sure that doesn't happen. Do what you have to do and I will take care of Clark. We'll take him and the boys somewhere safe."

"Thank you." I wrap my arms around her. We hold each other for a long time until I pull away and nod. "I'll do it. I'll make sure Cole doesn't get away with it."

CHAPTER 38

❦

After spending the night in a small room above The Night Owl, I find the courage to call the Willow Creek Police Department. When I reveal who I am, I'm promptly transferred to a man named Dan Mason, the lead detective. I guess only he is qualified to deal with such a high-profile case.

He asks me to come in. I refuse because there's no guarantee they won't arrest me.

"I'm calling to tell you that my father-in-law is not only guilty of raping those women, but he also murdered my husband and our housekeeper, and I will find the proof."

I'll only show my face to the police when I have the evidence that would help them arrest Cole and exonerate me. If the police were not able to find any evidence at the hotel or the house that I used to call my own, there's one other place they have not checked, a place they may not even know exists.

The moment Cole mentioned the cabin to Clark, I knew that was probably where he had been hiding. Whatever evidence I'm looking for might also be there.

As soon as I hang up the phone, I get on a bus out of town. The clock has just struck 6:00 p.m. when I hop onto a bus headed for Rustdale, the small town where Cole's cabin is located. To get there, though, I'll have to pass through Fort Haven.

Three hours later, the bus drives through the town I thought I'd never see again. The lights are warm and inviting, but I will never feel at home there again. It will forever be tainted in my mind.

It hurts to be traveling without Clark, but Tasha convinced me that it's safer this way, and it would make it easier for me to make quick decisions. I agreed. What I'm doing could also have put both of us in danger.

This is something I need to do alone, and I trust Tasha. She promised me she would take great care of my son. I'm pretty sure Cole's main priority is coming after me first, and that means Clark is safe from him for now. If Cole gets rid of me, that's another story.

Around 10:00 p.m. the bus stutters to a halt in Rustdale. It's a struggle to get to my feet because my knees are so weak with nerves.

I'm carrying only my handbag. Everything else we owned was left in the motel room since we left in such a hurry.

But it's good for me to travel light.

My hair is styled differently, and I have changed my eye color again. I look different in a pair of clothes that Tasha's brother has given me. They belong to his girlfriend. Leather pants with a jean jacket and a matching cap are not something I would normally wear, but I'm ready to step out of my comfort zone.

I'm someone else now. I have been scarred, broken, and crushed. There's barely anything of the old me left behind. The only part that remains is the one that loves my son, the one that's willing to fight for him, to fight to get our lives back.

Everything else has been destroyed by Cole and Brett.

"Ma'am, are you getting off?" a pregnant woman asks from behind me.

"Sorry," I murmur when I realize I'm blocking the way. I get off the bus. When it drives off, I halt, suddenly afraid. I came all this way, but now I'm unsure of exactly what I'm looking for and if I'll find it.

What if I find nothing to prove Cole committed the murders?

I still can't figure out why he killed Janella.

Did she really catch him killing Brett or is there more to this story that I'm not aware of?

As I wander around the bus stop, I try to figure it out. When Janella's face appears in my mind, the answers come rushing to me.

She was a sad woman, but she was very beautiful. Like all the women who worked as maids at the Black Oyster Hotel. What if Cole or Brett did the same things to her? What if she was also their victim?

The urge to vomit hits me so hard that I throw up my disgust into a nearby bush. A woman walking by curses under her breath and distances herself from me. I'm too far gone to care what anyone thinks of me vomiting in a public place.

It makes sense to think that Janella was also molested by Cole or Brett. If they were capable of abusing their employees at the hotel, what would stop them from abusing her?

Maybe that day, she warned Cole that she was going to the police. Maybe he saw no other way to protect himself but to kill her before she exposed him.

They did it. I feel it. And it was happening right under my roof. Every part of my body knows that I'm right.

When I moved into the house, she had probably already been victimized. That's why she never smiled. She was hurting.

I feel so dizzy that I need a moment to collect myself.

The dark street is deserted with only the occasional person walking by. I had planned on staying at a hotel first and going to the cabin in the morning, but I can no longer wait. Cole has been walking free long enough.

I straighten up, push my shoulders back, and wipe my mouth with a napkin from my handbag. I might feel weak inside, but nothing will stop me from seeking justice.

I need to find evidence that will nail him once and for all. Brett is not alive to pay for his crimes, so Cole will have to pay for both. He has to go to prison. He has to hurt, to experience how it feels to be stripped of everything you knew, everything you cherished.

The Brittle Rose cabin is in the woods, at least twenty minutes from the bus stop, so I take a taxi. It's also safer than walking.

During the drive, the taxi driver plays a few gospel songs on the radio. I wish they could soothe me, but only Cole's arrest would do that. Still, I close my eyes and allow the music to wash over me.

"Sir, would you mind waiting for me?" I ask when we arrive. I don't want to be out here all alone.

I gaze out the window into the darkness. Everything is pitch black. I don't know if the spare key is still kept in the same spot as last time. If not, it doesn't matter. I'll find a way to get inside. I will break the windows if I have to.

"No problem." The man reaches for his headphones on the passenger's seat. "Take all the time you need. But it will cost extra."

"That's fine," I say. I always walk around with my cash, keeping every penny I own near me in case something happens, and I have to run.

Outside the taxi, the air is cool against my skin. It smells of flowers and pine. I remember loving the smells the one time I came with Brett. But this time, the fresh scents are laced with a note of danger.

I make my way to the front door, glancing behind me to make sure the taxi is still waiting.

To my surprise, the key is still in its usual place underneath a potted plant on the porch.

In contrast to outside, the air inside is heavy, old, and tainted. Something is not right, and I feel it. I switch on the lights and it floods the luxurious cabin.

The leather couch, massage chair, and expensive throw pillows and rugs make it a perfect bachelor escape. Some might find the place relaxing, but not me, not anymore. Standing inside it, I get a bitter tang in my mouth and an impulse to flee.

A chilly black silence surrounds the place, daring me to disturb it. I'm dreading what it hides from the world. What secrets it's harboring. I suddenly feel ill-equipped to take on this dangerous task, but it's too late to turn back and I refuse to leave empty-handed.

I dive into it without hesitation. There's no time to waste. This might be my only chance to make things right for everyone who suffered at the hands of Cole Wilton.

The power of hate is racing through my veins, giving me the courage I need to face the unknown.

I want to be his greatest mistake ever. I want to make him regret the day he hired me, and especially the day he laid a hand on me.

CHAPTER 39

❧

The cabin has two bedrooms in total, but only one seems functional. The other is bare from floor to ceiling. Aside from the paneled walls and dark floorboards, there's nothing inside it.

I rub my arms to erase the goosebumps on my skin. Even the air is devoid of warmth.

The last and only time I was at the cabin, we slept in the room that's now empty. I would like to think Cole removed everything from it that had reminded him of Brett, because it hurt too much, but I know better. He had no love whatsoever for his son.

Since there's nothing to see, I step out of the room and head to the other bedroom. It has the same feel to it as Cole's suite at the Black Oyster.

As I stand in the doorway, my gaze taking in the vintage leather couch by the window that overlooks a lake, and the king-sized bed, it's hard for me to breathe. It reminds me of the hotel and everything that happened there.

I brace myself and step farther into the room. Searching it doesn't take long. There's nothing to find. The room may be furnished, but it's still empty. The only thing in the closet is an empty designer suitcase. The drawers have been emptied, and the bathroom cabinets are bare.

I search the rest of the cabin and come across a cupboard in the living room with three rifles propped up inside it. I step back, a heavy feeling settling in my stomach. I shut it again. Guns make me nervous.

I hear something slamming, and I rush to the window in a panic. I'm relieved to see only the taxi driver. He's smoking a cigarette outside his car. The sound I heard was probably of him shutting the car door.

I drop the curtain and turn back to the room.

Maybe this was a mistake. I came all this way without a clear plan of exactly what I was looking for. It's not surprising that I didn't find it. The best thing for me to do is probably to get out, but my hunger for revenge has me in a vice and refuses to let go.

I need to bring Cole to justice so Clark and I can rebuild our lives without a dark cloud over our heads. The thought of running again exhausts me. Clark is the reason I search the cabin again. I need to prove Cole is guilty of murder, so I can be free to raise my son without fear.

My son. Not Cole's. Not Brett's.

I search every room again, including the kitchen, where I find an unfinished mug of coffee on the counter. It makes me suspect that Cole was at the cabin recently. I need to search faster and get the hell out.

I don't care that I'm moving things out of their usual places. Maybe a part of me wants him to know I was in the cabin.

My search leads to nothing. It's as if someone came and scrubbed the place clean, taking away all the secrets, leaving only tainted air and the scent of evil behind.

I return to the empty room, standing in the middle, turning from one side to the other, wondering if there's something I'm missing, something I can't see. I've searched every nook, and yet I feel as if there's something else hiding in the shadows.

I pace the floor from one end to the other and run my hands along the walls. No success.

There's nothing here. It was foolish of me to think Cole would be so careless to leave evidence lying around in plain sight, especially since the key to the cabin was also easily accessible.

I need to get out of the place, to head to the only hotel in town, and get some sleep. My head will be clearer in the morning and I will be able to make better decisions. I might have to get the cops involved. If I notify them of the cabin's existence and location, they might be able to find something. But I won't be here when they arrive. I won't let them come near me until Cole is considered to be the prime murder suspect.

Biting hard on my lower lip, I slump against one of the walls, drop my handbag to the floor and slide down next to it. I draw my knees to my body and hug them, resting my forehead against them.

After sitting on the floor for a while, too weak to get up, I remember that the taxi driver is waiting for me outside. If I don't want to pay a fortune, I have to go.

As I shift my weight, struggling to get to my feet, the floor creaks underneath me.

On my hands and knees, I crawl around the area. It's not unusual for a floor to creak, but since I'm hunting for any clue that could lead me to the truth, a floorboard creaking could mean something different to me than it would someone else.

I spring to my feet and start hopping at random places in the room. Only a quarter of the room has creaking floorboards.

My heart is pounding in my ears when I get to my hands and knees again and feel the floor for more clues, slamming my fists into it.

One of my nails snaps when I insert it between two slabs of wood, so I grab a knife from the kitchen to get the job done. Finally, one of the boards is loosened enough to reveal what's hidden from the world.

My instinct was right. I'm staring at the top of a brown box that has been taped shut.

I get to work removing more of the floorboards to get full access to the box. There's more than one box. I'm seeing at least three, all of them taped shut.

Sweat is dripping from my forehead as I cut through the tape and start opening the first box without lifting it from its hiding place.

It's full of DVDs in white cases, at least a dozen of them. The spines of the cases are labeled with numbers.

102. 201. 300. Only one of them has words.

Honeymoon suite

My chest tingles with dread.

It doesn't take a genius to figure out what I'm staring at. The DVDs are not random numbers. They're room numbers.

Cole is one sick bastard. He must have recorded people in their hotel rooms.

Grabbing several DVDs, I get to my feet. I'll watch them at the hotel and call the cops to get the rest. I'm about to leave the room when I spot another DVD in the box. The label on it catches my eye.

Master bedroom

I grab it as well.

I should leave now, but now that I've discovered the place that might contain all the evidence, it would be a mistake to get out without covering up my tracks. If Cole shows up, I don't want him to know immediately that I found his hiding place and move the stuff before the police get to it.

I do my best to spread out the rest of the DVDs in the box to create a flat surface, then slide the floorboards back into their place as best I can.

I need to act fast. I can't go to the hotel first. I haven't watched the DVDs yet, but my heart tells me they have all the evidence I've been searching for. I need to call the police right away. I'll wait in the taxi for them to arrive.

What if there's nothing on the DVDs?

The thought makes me rethink my decision. What if it was a trap and the DVDs have nothing on them? If I call the police, I could

337

end up being the one thrown behind bars.

But I can't shake the feeling that the DVDs hold the answers, that they're the key to my freedom.

To be on the safe side, I decide that I'll call the cops and drive to the hotel to wait for whatever comes next. If they find something, it would be all over the news and I'd know whether or not I should come out of hiding.

I reach for my handbag and rummage inside for my phone while gazing out the window to make sure the taxi is still outside. It's still there, but I don't see the driver. Dread creeps up on me as I bring my face closer to the glass to better search the darkness.

I don't see it coming. I don't hear a thing. I only feel the pain that flares at the back of my skull. The bag drops to the floor and I follow it down, my head colliding with the floorboard.

My eyes start to close but not before I see a man coming into view. Even through my blurred vision, I'm able to identify him.

Cole is wearing the cab driver's cap.

"I knew you would come." His voice cuts the silence. He sounds so distant and muffled, but the words are clear. "I left the key for you."

It was a trap, after all.

As I drift in and out of consciousness, it occurs to me that he only mentioned the cabin to Clark at the motel because he wanted to remind me of its existence. He wanted to lure me to it. He figured out my plan even before me. He was a few steps ahead.

The sound of the floorboards creaking as he walks makes my head hurt even more, like there are fiery explosions going off inside of it.

Something smashes against the wall. I can't tell whether it's one of the DVDs. I want to look, but the pain has rendered me immobile.

I'm still trying to push through the pain in my head when more pain explodes in me—this time in my middle. He's kicked me. Now I'm falling hard and fast into the darkness.

"My son," I whisper, but I'm unable to say more.

"I know where he is," Cole calls out. "When all this is over, I'll bring him here. We'll go hunting together. I'll teach him how to be a man. I failed with Brett, but I have a chance to try again."

"No," I croak. I want to stay and fight for my son. When I lift my arm a few inches off the floor, it falls back down. My strength is seeping out of me, leaving me deflated.

It's over. I failed Clark. I failed myself.

My eyes close.

CHAPTER 40

❧

My eyes fly open and my lungs suck in air. No matter how greedy I am, how much I gulp in, it's not enough.

Everything is dark except for a blinking red light above me, very close to my face.

When I try to stretch my arms out, they meet a soft surface, some kind of fabric. I force my mind to push through the pain and figure out where I am.

"Welcome back," Cole says. "Be still. Try not to panic or you'll run out of air."

It wasn't a nightmare. He *did* find me. This time, he'll never let me go. He'll kill me, and I'll never see Clark again.

A hot tear slides down the side of my face.

"I planned this moment for a year," he continues. "I always knew it would end like this."

"What..." I can't speak because my mouth is so dry, and my head is on the verge of exploding.

"Where, you mean? Well, you're inside your pretty coffin. I had it custom-made for you."

My body stiffens and panic like I've never known before flares up inside me.

He has buried me alive?

"No," I say, but the words only come out in a whisper. "No," I repeat even though it hurts to speak.

"It will be much harder if you resist it. My suggestion is that you should enjoy your last doses of oxygen. Your supply is limited."

"Let me out," I shout. "Please, Cole."

"That's not going to happen."

This is my worst nightmare.

When I was six, my parents died in a mall that had collapsed. Ever since, I've been afraid of being buried alive. I found out years later that they did not die from being crushed, but from suffocating underneath the rubble. They were found four days later after taking who knows how long to die. That thought has haunted me all my life.

Once I told Brett that if I died, I wanted to be cremated to ensure I was really dead. I'd read horror stories of people who woke up in their coffins and ended up dying from lack of oxygen.

Now my life is doomed to end in exactly the

way I'd feared.

My mind goes back to Clark, and I remember Cole telling me that he knows his location. I hope he was only trying to scare me. If he was busy coming after me, how would he know where Tasha took him? Unless of course, he paid someone to follow them.

"Don't hurt my son," I say, fresh tears burning my eyes.

"Don't worry, our son will be safe. I'll toughen him up a bit. I don't want him to end up like Brett did."

I can't let him do it. I can't let him destroy Clark.

"He's not yours," I shout, pressing against the silky coffin lining. My will to fight rewards me with a huge dose of adrenaline that I use to push against the top of the coffin.

Nothing moves.

"Push harder." He laughs. "Just a little harder."

I don't know if he's playing games with me, but he doesn't need to tell me to push harder because I already am. I won't go down without a fight.

To my surprise, the cover pops open and air rushes into my lungs. It smells of rotten leaves and wet earth.

It's still dark outside, but it was darker inside

the closed coffin. I scramble to my feet to get out of the coffin, my skin crawling. Dizziness makes me fall back in, so I crawl out instead and lie next to it on the damp ground, panting as I look up at the moonlight that slices through the leaves of the trees above.

Move. Save yourself.

Wherever he is, Cole is watching. I'm the prey, and he's waiting to pounce. He released me from the coffin so he can have fun chasing me before he ends my life.

First, I roll to my side and then onto my hands and knees.

I almost fall into a deep hole next to the coffin.

I swallow a scream as I kick my feet into the ground and use my hands to move me away from the grave he's dug for me. If I don't save myself, I'll end up back inside the coffin, six feet under.

I struggle to my feet, ignoring the pain roiling through my body.

When I start to run blindly into the trees, gulping in the smell of decomposing wood, his laughter rings out around me. My body is weak, but I keep going, breaking twigs with my bare feet and jumping over logs. I fall a couple of times, but I pick myself up again.

It's only when my lungs start to burn that I

343

stop to listen, to try and determine how far away he is. I no longer hear his voice. The only sound is that of the river.

But not for long.

The sound of pounding feet alerts me that he's running after me.

He refuses to let me get away. If he didn't have a limp, he would probably have caught up with me already.

I need to lose him. I don't know where I'm going. I don't know if he has a trap waiting for me ahead, or if I might end up being attacked by wild animals, but I need to keep moving.

A gunshot slices the night and I fall to the ground as if I have been hit by the bullet. When I realize I'm fine, I get back on my feet again and continue.

"You won't get far," he says behind me. He's using a megaphone. I don't know how far he is now. I can't turn to look. It will only slow me down.

I keep running until the pain in my chest threatens to stop me, but I push my body to its limit. The trees are both my friends and enemies. They hide me, but their thorns and branches also cut into my skin. I don't care. Pain is better than death.

"Run, Meghan, run," he booms. "Run like Brett used to when I chased him like an animal.

He was a coward even as a kid."

My breath catches in my throat.

Is this what he did to his son, what he wants to do to mine?

"Hunting was supposed to teach him how to be a man. He was the animal and I was the prey. I always caught up. He never told you, did he?"

I struggle to recover from the emotional blow that accompanies Cole's words, but I need to keep running. I want to stop, to throw up. But that's not an option.

My feet continue to pound the earth, but I feel myself slowing down. My body is reaching its limit, and there's not much I can do about it. His confession has served its purpose. It has weakened me.

Another bullet splits the silence only moments before a sharp pain strikes my right leg. I bite back a scream when the force of impact stops me in my tracks.

It's game over.

Brett once came home with a wound in his leg. He told me there was an accident and he refused to go to the hospital. Now I know the truth. His father had shot him, too.

I fall to the ground, writhing with pain. Still determined to get away, I bury my nails into the soil, begging it to move me forward. But nothing happens.

I can make out his footfalls now. He's getting closer, closer, closer.

By the time he reaches me, I'm barely conscious. My eyes close as soon as he lifts me from the ground. They only open again when we arrive at the cabin.

I try to squirm from his grip, but he's strong. He doesn't speak as he drops me into a chair in the living room in front of the TV.

Blood is seeping from my wound. I feel it sliding down the back of my leg to the floor, as my weak body slumps to the side.

He pushes me upright again and ties something around my chest, a rope maybe.

There's not an ounce of strength left in my body to fight him.

"You came looking for answers," he whispers into my ear. "You're about to get them in brilliant color." When my head lolls forward, he grips my hair and turns my face back to the screen, which is now flickering to life.

My eyes are blurry, but I am forcing myself to watch my life unfolding in front of me.

I'm watching a video of him falling over me in the hotel room the night before my wedding. He has the rape on video. The raw anguish spills out of me in a low moan as my wounded heart demands the revenge that it may never find.

After what seems like an eternity, he changes the DVD. The next one is of me and Brett in our bedroom, making love.

He was watching us the entire time. He listened to every one of our conversations. That must be how he heard me tell Brett that I was terrified of being buried alive. He wanted to bring my worst fears to life.

In the DVD after that, Brett is asking me to help him die. Cole has a grin on his face, but he doesn't say a word as he slides in another DVD. He's only showing me snippets, only what he wants me to see.

I watch my husband on screen, lying in bed, and begging me to take him out of his misery. I listen to myself telling him I can't do it and fleeing from the room.

The TV goes blank.

"I knew you wouldn't go through with it." Cole puts the DVDs back in their cases.

"So, you killed your own son." My eyes are blazing at him now. The physical pain is forgotten, distant, as if it belongs to someone else.

"It's a good thing he died, Meghan. It was time. He was useless to me and to you. He was my biggest mistake." He shakes his head. "All my life I tried to cleanse him, turn him from the son of a dead prostitute to a respectable, powerful, and strong man. I never wanted the boy, but I was curious to see if I could turn him into me. I guess I failed."

Brett never told me that his mother was a prostitute. He never wanted to talk about her. He only mentioned that she left him when he was a child.

Cole tilts his head to the side. "Now that you have the truth you came searching for, it's time for you to die. Your coffin is waiting." He unties the rope from around my body.

I don't know what gets into me, but I jump to my feet, prepared to escape. It's foolish. He has too much power over me for it to work.

"Don't you dare come near me, you monster." Even though my body is vibrating with adrenaline, my wounded leg refuses to play along. I limp to the back of the chair, daring him to approach me.

"Stop resisting, Meghan. It's over now. No one can save you out here." He pulls a silver handgun from his back pocket and takes a step toward me.

When he comes closer, I use the little strength I have left to lift the chair, swinging it as hard as I can in his direction. It strikes him on the left side of his body. He growls and drops his gun, but otherwise he doesn't flinch.

Both our gazes move to the weapon on the floor. It's closer to me than to him. Since I can't walk, I fall over it. He lunges for me as my fingers curl around the gun.

"Goodbye, Meghan." He grabs my hair and drives my head into the floor before snatching the gun from my hand.

Before my eyes can close, I hear a gunshot.

CHAPTER 41

〜

I thought I'd never wake up again, but I do. I can still smell him. His presence is suffocating me, but I can't see him.

"Where am I?" I ask even though I'm not sure if anyone is with me.

"You're in the hospital," a woman's voice says. It's familiar, but I have to wade through the mess inside my head to place it. When I do, my eyes fill with tears.

"Tasha," I whisper, choking up.

"Are you okay, Zoe?" She comes to my bedside, her eyes sparkling. My vision is blurred, but it's starting to clear.

Without moving my head, which still hurting, I scan the room. I can tell from the pressure around it that it's bandaged, as is my leg.

"Where is Clark? Where is my son?"

"Don't worry." Tasha strokes my cheek. "Clark is fine. He's safe. So are you."

"Where is he? Where's...Cole?" I'd heard a bullet. Did I manage to shoot him? Did he shoot me?

"He was shot by the police." She wipes her cheek. "They got to him just in time. If they came even a second later, he could have killed you."

I blink at her, confused. How could the police have shot Cole when they were not at the cabin?

"He's dead?" I bite into my trembling bottom lip.

"No, Mrs. Wilton," a man answers from the doorway. "But you never have to worry about him again." He stretches out a hand to shake mine. "I'm detective Jason Rogers."

The forty-something detective is tall with pale skin, red hair, and eyes so dark they look black.

"You saved my life?" I squeeze his hand.

"No, a taxi driver called the police. He said he drove you to the cabin, and Cole Wilton stabbed him with a knife. Unfortunately, he didn't make it. But if it weren't for him, you might not have either."

Another person is dead because of me. That's all I can think as I listen to what the detective is telling me. He gives me the time I need to cry for the man who saved my life.

Tasha strokes my back in silence.

"Cole did it," I say finally. "He also killed my husband, Brett Wilton, and our housekeeper. There were DVDs."

"We know that."

"Was my husband's murder recorded?"

The detective shakes his head. "No, but he admitted to being involved in your husband's murder."

"I'm innocent." I hold on to Tasha's hand, overcome with emotion.

The man nods with a smile. "You are innocent of murder, yes."

*

Three hours after I speak to Detective Rogers, Clark steps into my hospital room. He's holding a teddy bear I haven't seen before.

"Mommy, Mommy." He rushes to my bedside. With tears in his eyes, he places his little hand on my forehead. "Don't die."

"No." I smile through my tears. "That won't happen. I'm not going anywhere."

The detective said that since there was evidence that I *did* intend to kill Brett, and even had the deadly medication prepared, I could still be charged. However, I spoke to a lawyer over the phone, who promised to do everything to clear my name of any charges. She doubted I would end up in prison.

"What's that?" I ask about an object Clark is holding in his other hand.

"It's a syringe. The nurse gave it to me. But it's not a real injection."

"Do you want to make Mommy better?" I ask, remembering the game he used to play with Brett.

His face goes blank and he shakes his head. "I don't want to." His voice is trembling now.

"Why not? You can pretend you're the doctor. I'm your patient."

"But I don't want you to leave and go to heaven."

I frown. "Baby, what do you mean? I won't go anywhere."

"But daddy did."

"Yes, because he was very sick. He was in a lot of pain."

Clark nods and drops his head. "I wanted to make his pain go away, but he went to get better in heaven."

"You tried to make it go away?" A cold shower of realization hits me. "What are you saying?"

After a long silence, he speaks. "Grandpa said if I inject daddy, he will not have pain anymore. He will go to heaven and rest. He said we are daddy's secret angels." Clark puts a finger on his lips. "Shhh, don't tell anyone."

"Okay, I won't." I sit up and the room starts to spin. "You... you tried to make daddy better? You injected him?"

"Grandpa gave me the injection. He said I had to be brave for daddy. He said I am a big man."

"Did he show you how to do it?" My mouth feels like dry, dusty paper.

Clark nods. "He helped me. I pushed the thing in the injection and daddy got the medicine." He crawls up to lie next to me in the hospital bed. When I wrap my arms around him, I'm trembling.

It suddenly occurs to me why Cole always said he was involved in Brett's murder, but he never actually said he killed him.

That's because he made somebody else do it. He made my son, a child, commit the murder. Cole was the one who had left Clark's door open that night.

EPILOGUE
One Year Later

∼⌒∽

I sit on the grass, enjoying the touch of the breeze as it sweeps through my hair. The blades of grass underneath my feet feel like heaven.

"I want more juice," Clark says and I smile, reaching for his plastic cup.

The picnic was his idea. He hates being indoors, and I understand. Now that he's free to be a kid again, we spend a lot of time outdoors making up for lost time.

At a distance, several children are playing. A few minutes ago, Clark played with some of them. Seeing him play with other children warmed my heart and broke it at the same time.

He's still a child like them, but at the same time, he has been robbed of his innocence.

No matter how many years go by, I will remember what Cole did to him.

My fear now is that Clark will never forget that night. And if he does forget, there will come a day when he will want to know how his father died. Brett was for sure his father. A DNA test proved that Clark was not Cole's.

Cole is the one who went to prison for Brett's murder, among other things, because he was the mastermind and the adult. One day, though, Clark will be old enough to ask the hard questions and understand what his grandfather made him do.

At his sentencing, Cole shocked the entire courtroom when he shouted that he may be in prison, but he still lives on in Clark and that he will continue his legacy one day. In my mind, I immediately shut down his comment. I was determined to do everything possible to make sure my son never followed in Cole's footsteps.

In the courtroom and the newspapers, I discovered a lot of things about Cole's childhood that he never told anyone about. Although it doesn't excuse his behavior, I now understand why he chose to become the man he was. He was born and raised in Beaufort, South Carolina, by a father who was an oyster farmer, and a mother who physically and emotionally abused them both. His mother was responsible for the injury that resulted in his limp, when she broke his leg with a spade.

He had just finished high school when his father finally stood up to his wife, killing her, and then himself. Cole left Beaufort after their deaths and went to the University of Florida. He graduated with honors and later worked for a major luxury hotel chain until he decided to open up his Black Oyster chain of hotels, where he raped women to punish them for his late mother's cruelty. His past may also have been the reason he is against marriage. He probably believes that it's the thing that weakens men, just as it did his father.

I push Cole to the back of my mind. A past, however dark, does not give anyone the license to kill and harm others.

All I care about is that the slate has been wiped clean. The court has declared both me and Clark not guilty, and we can live our lives without fear. For Clark's sake, I'm learning to embrace life, even with the scars on my heart.

When Clark finishes his drink, he hugs me and runs off to play some more.

His laughter floats back to me when he chases after a girl with pigtails. It's so pure, untainted, but for how long?

I shake my head. I can't think about it now. When the time comes, I'll be there to hold him. I will do everything in my power to make sure he knows it was not his fault, that he was manipulated.

I throw back my head and gaze up at the sky,

watching the clouds moving and forming shapes.

I think of Cole behind bars. He's in a high-security prison, serving a life sentence with no chance of parole. His sentencing was easy, especially when Marjorie finally came to her senses and admitted that she had lied for him. With no other defense, Cole confessed to killing Janella and also Denise. They had both threatened to go to the cops to report that he had raped them.

Roland, the corrupt police officer, was caught and jailed, but he was killed by another inmate while awaiting trial.

A week after Cole was locked up forever, Clark and I returned to Willow Creek to try to live a quiet life. It's our new home now. I decided to keep the name Zoe because the name Meghan was damaged by so much pain.

When Clark finishes playing, we get into our car and drive home.

Three months after Mrs. Foster's death, her lawyer showed up at my door and shocked me.

Mrs. Foster had left me everything she had owned. The house, some savings, and even the cabin all belong to me now. Maybe deep down, she knew I was innocent. I used some of the money to open up Heaven's Cakes Bakery, located on the same street as Lemon, where I deliver freshly baked goods every morning. Owning my own bakery or restaurant was something I've always dreamed of, and I know it would make Mrs. Foster proud.

It still feels strange now to walk down the path from the gate to the front door. Sometimes I expect Mrs. Foster to walk out.

When Clark is playing video games in his room after lunch, I go to my bedroom and switch on my computer.

After being approached many times by publishers, I'm finally ready to write a book.

It's almost done, but I left the title for last. With only one chapter left to go, I finally type it in.

The Widow's Cabin

It's perfect.

I position my hands on the keyboard again and start to write the epilogue.

Before I can finish, I glance at a box in the corner and my eyes land on a manila envelope I had been dreading to open for a year.

Maybe I'm ready for that too.

The envelope was in a secret safe in the house, just as Brett told me it would be. He said if the cops ever started thinking I was a murderer, it would contain everything I needed to disappear. I had expected to find money and fake passports inside, but when I finally got my hands on it, I knew it was too thin.

I spill the contents onto the bed, but only one sheet of paper slides out. It's a letter.

Perplexed, I pick it up.

Meghan,

I'm sure you thought you would find something different, something to help you run from the law if the cops find out you killed me. I'm sorry to disappoint you. I cannot give you the escape you need. I asked you to kill me for a reason. It was all in the name of revenge.

The truth is out, Meghan. I know what you did with my father the night before our wedding. He told me everything. He showed me photos. You probably know by now that I did some terrible things, things I'm not proud of. What you don't know is that you changed me. When I met you, I became a different man, a better man. I gave up my old ways.

I thought you were different, but I was wrong. Like any other woman, you were defenseless to my father's charms. What hurts the most is that you never told me.

That's why I did it. I wanted you to commit murder and go to prison. Does that make me evil? I guess it does. I am, after all, my father's son. Speaking of sons, my father told me Liam is not mine, but his. Did you think I'd never find out?

My father is an evil man, but the one thing he did right in his life is showing me the true colors of the woman I married. I'll stop here. There's nothing more to say.

I'd like to wish you a good life, but I'd be lying if I say I want you to be happy. The opposite is true.

I drop the letter to the floor, my mind spinning and my heart breaking all over again.

I know the day Cole told Brett the truth. It was the day he was called out for an emergency and came back a changed man, when he started pulling away from me and Clark. It was the night he asked me to help him die.

"Mommy, Mommy," Clark calls. "There's a squirrel in our garden. Come and look."

"I'm coming." I bite down on my lip until it stings.

In a daze, I get to my feet, barely able to hold myself up. On my way outside, I reread the letter inside my mind. I'm too shocked to even cry.

I make it to the garden in one piece and pretend to be excited about the squirrel.

Then I return to my room to add the letter to the last chapter of my book. The case may be closed, but I will still make the letter public to further exonerate myself in case there's anyone out there who ever doubted my innocence.

In the evening, Tasha comes over with her

kids for a movie and pizza. The moment she enters the house, I'm reminded that even after what I discovered, I can still choose to be free. I'm free to start over, to create a better future for myself and Clark.

Brett and his father no longer have power over me. They do not get to have the last word. I do.

THE END

Thank you for reading The Widow's Cabin. If you enjoyed the books, please take time to review.

To be notified when L.G. Davis releases a new book, sign up for her newsletter at http://www.author-lgdavis.com.

Other books by L.G. Davis

Don't Blink
The Midnight Wife
The Stolen Breath

To get in touch with L.G. Davis visit:
www.author-lgdavis.com
Email: Liz@lizgdavis.com

Made in the USA
Coppell, TX
25 November 2020